a dream life

claire messud

tablo
tales

TABLO TALES

Tablo Tales is an imprint of Tablo Publishing.
First published in 2021 by Tablo Tales.
Level 1, 41–43 Stewart St, Richmond VIC 3121
www.tablo.com

21 22 23 LSC 10 9 8 7 6 5 4 3 2 1

A Dream Life

ISBN: 9781649697295

All profits are to go to WIRES Wildlife Rescue, an Australian
wildlife rescue & rehabilitation charity organisation.

Cover design by Alissa Dinallo
Set in 12/16.5pt Adobe Garamond Pro by Midland Typesetters, Australia

tablo

tales

For Margaret Riches Messud
and
for Elizabeth Messud

Sydney, 1971

The American family rented the house without having seen it – how could they have, halfway around the world? – so they did not know what it meant. When the limousine that had brought them from the airport pulled up before the gates, when it turned into the circular drive, around the trickling fountain, at the foot of which bloomed an open mouth of waxy red begonias, and came to a halt beneath the ivy-trailed, sand-coloured portico, the husband smiled, a half-smile which did not reveal his teeth, and, his eyebrows raised, murmured, "Oh, my."

The two little girls in the back seat rubbed at their eyes and tugged their crumpled frocks. "Are we here, Mom? Is this it?" asked the elder, a child of six. Her sister, a few weeks past her fourth birthday, stared at the lion's-head knockers on the dark, double-fronted door and slipped a consoling thumb into her mouth. But their mother said nothing at all.

Sir Robert and his Lady, Maureen, had built the house after the fortune was earned — waste and haulage, not mentioned in company — but before the knighthood had been bestowed. In his lighter moments, Sir Robert (a man without pretensions, in spite of his relatively recent wealth; a virtue not shared by his spouse) was wont to jest that it was the house, rather than his business accomplishments, which had brought them the reward of a title. And the house, it was true, was fit for a Lord, a British manor house in miniature, squeezed onto a large but nevertheless urban lot in an admired inner-Sydney neighbourhood, within spitting distance (another of Sir Robert's observations) of the sea.

The house sat at a fork between two quiet streets along which extended rows of somewhat more modest structures. Its grounds were thus essentially triangular, with the gate at their narrowest point, and high, pink-and-white brick walls along the roads on either side; and within those walls, to Maureen's specifications, Sir Robert had contrived to create space not only for the imposing building – like the walls, of pink-and-white brick, softened by greenery – with its grand portico, but also for a separate double-fronted garage designed to resemble stables; and for a rose garden and a wide sloping swathe of manicured lawn; and for an area of small fruit trees in military rows near the back wall, coyly referred to as 'the orchard'; and for a walled vegetable garden, along one side of which stretched a large wire enclosure known as 'My Lady's Aviary'.

In their early days in the house, Lady Maureen (nee O'Mara, the red-haired daughter of a bank clerk from Katoomba) had taken a keen interest in the walled garden, and in her birds – a trio of galahs and a sulphur-crested cockatoo, bestowed upon her by her doting husband – but the vegetables she had planted failed to flourish, and the birds, one by screeching one, had sickened and died, to the great relief of the neighbours (among them a genteel piano teacher with an exceedingly sensitive ear). By the time Sir Robert accepted the invitation to spend several years overseeing a complex waste-management project in far-off Manchester, England, Lady Maureen had long since given over all care of the garden to Davy Jones, the gardener, and was not sorry to leave the forlorn aviary, testament to a brief folly, behind.

Lady Maureen had been less content to abandon her beloved house to strangers, but Sir Robert was a practical man – Deeds was his name, the son of a construction worker, and so Australian to the core that he claimed convict ancestry on both sides – and would not allow it to sit empty.

"A little extra income never goes amiss, Mo," he insisted, one night after supper, in the conservatory, as they watched the sun set over Sydney Harbour. He rolled and sniffed a plump cigar, and clamped it between his yellow teeth.

"Renters, though, Bob – think of it." Lady Maureen puffed her cheeks and scowled.

"A high class of renter, Mo. Such things exist. They'll keep the burglars out. Think of that."

And when Lady Maureen thought of that, of thick grubby fingers rifling through her linen cupboards, of clumsy louts stuffing burlap sacks full of Deeds booty – the china shepherdesses and the silver plate – or bashing at the Bechstein (which she did not, herself, know how to play) – when she thought of that, she conceded, only insisting that her husband have his agent personally vet the prospective tenants, and that she herself would never have to know the first thing about them, not their names nor their number nor their activities. In this way, she told herself, she could pretend that they did not exist, in the same way she shut out of her memory the noisy little bungalow in which she had grown up, and her early stint at the glove counter in Grace Bros department store; the way she ignored, by a trick of mirrors, her own thickened waistline, and with the assistance of careful corsetry denied the increasing droop of her bosom. (Her face, less easy to hide from, a broad face with a small forehead and a propensity for jowls, she would deal with while abroad, in more radical fashion, under the knife in an exclusive Swiss clinic.)

*

The Americans were dumbfounded by their new home. The four of them had left behind a cramped two-bedroom apartment on New York's Upper East Side, whose chief advantage had been the view, available from the kitchen window with much bobbing and craning, of a silver swatch of the East River, caught between two massive modern buildings like their own. The little girls had never known anything else, had considered houses with staircases and unfolding rooms to be a novelty of grandparenthood: their mother's parents, in Buffalo, lived in such a place, while their father's mother had sold her marital home upon her husband's death and retreated to a small apartment, not unlike theirs, in Chicago.

Upon arrival, then, in the Deeds residence ("Chateau Deeds", as the father jokingly dubbed it, a name that would live in their family lore forever), the two girls ran squealing from room to room; they clattered along the broad parquet hall and peered into the great drawing room, with its alcove study and foggy drapes; into the panelled dining room, the morning room, the library; they tumbled through the conservatory in a giggling sweep, and back to the hall, where they paused in bafflement at the green baize door until their mother pushed it ajar, allowing them the run of the back of the house – the kitchen, the pantry, the coat room, the laundry room, so many shiny floors upon which little feet might create a thundering roar. They tripped up the back staircase to the servants' apartment and the sewing room, and thence onto the second floor, where they found the studded trunks full of their clothes and toys awaiting, magically, in the nursery, beyond which extended a large sunlit playroom of their very own. Along the upstairs hall they discovered door upon door, enclosing bedroom upon bedroom, and at the end, near the elaborate, arced front staircase, their parents' room, a vastness of sky-blue carpet along which the tracks of the last vacuuming were still apparent. This master bedroom gave, through long and sparkling windows, onto the front garden and the drive, so that it held within it the constant murmur of the fountain; and beyond the walls, beyond the road and smaller houses so neatly arrayed, it gave onto the sea, no faint and tiny square barely glimpsed but a glittering expanse, across which ferries and little sailboats and occasional cargo ships skittered like insects.

While the girls leaned, that first time, against the glass, pressing their small fingerprints into its perfect surface, their father moved in the adjoining bathroom, running the taps, and their mother stood behind them, one arm to her ribs, the other clasping a cigarette, staring also out of the window, saying nothing.

"It's really something," said her husband, emerging, rubbing his face with a plum-coloured towel. "We've moved up in the world, sweetie, that's for sure."

"We've moved to the end of the earth is what we've done," she replied, stubbing her cigarette in a small mosaic ashtray among the knick-knacks on the dresser. "What time is it in New York?"

"It's yesterday," he said. "Imagine that! Like time travel."

"So we've lost a day," she said. "Gone from our lives – *poof.* Like that."

"Where'd it go, Mom?" asked the elder of her daughters, open-mouthed. "Where does a day go, without us?"

But her mother merely shrugged, and left the room.

*

Alice Armstrong had not welcomed her husband's promotion. When he first announced his posting to Sydney, she had bit her lip and said, "Are they moving you up or out, Teddy? Up or out?"

But he, with his uneven grin and his caterpillar brows awry, had barely heard, and had not understood. "Up, up and away," he cried, embracing her and trying to lead a waltz around their tiny kitchen. It was winter then, and through the window a dove-coloured dusk had fallen on the patch of river. The apartments all around were dotted with cozy yellow light, and in their distant windows, people, families, moved like shadow puppets. "First class all the way, sweetie. First class!" he marvelled, certain she must share his delight.

And she, finally, had struggled from his grasp, had patted his cheek with her cold hand. "I'm glad you're so happy. I'm glad it's the right thing for your career. I'd better go check on the girls."

Now, slipping like a ghost through the opulent rooms, Alice thought she understood where she was: in a dream life, where nothing could matter and nothing would last, a hiatus from reality which, precisely like time travel, would deposit her back on her own shores, in her own time, at some unforeseeable but anticipated moment. All this would be revealed to be a mirage, which was why her fear was unnecessary (although she could not quell it), why her anger was itself an illusion (although she could barely contain it), and why her eyes and limbs felt so very heavy, as though she dragged through sand.

What would make it real, this life? Her husband would have the bank, long hours with men scrubbed and eager as himself, would be juggling numbers, flirting with secretaries, bolstered in emphatic normality by the conferences, the jugs of water, pots of coffee, neat rows of pens and paper, the enclosed hum of air conditioning and the artificial lights. Her daughters would have school, the thrill of elaborate uniforms and square, plastic school cases, nametags on their socks and knickers, in the brims of their hats — straw for summer and felt for winter, secured with thick elastic beneath their plump, smooth chins. They would have teachers and playmates, schoolyard games of witches and fairies, and, in time, piano lessons at the elbow of the genteel teacher next door.

But she, Alice Armstrong, would have only Chateau Deeds, and, to be sure, on that first bleary morning as she opened doors and drawers and inspected the walled garden and the musty garage (in which Lady Maureen's rose-coloured Bentley loomed beneath a pearly tarpaulin), as she ran her hand along the pink-and-white bricks, rough and crumbly, at the side of the house, as she inhaled the salt breeze and strolled barefoot across the crispy side lawn to the shade of the miniature orchard, brushing away insects and hearing, as if from faraway, the singsong of her daughters' invented games – to be sure, on that day, Alice Armstrong could not know what that meant.

She had, in New York, all her adult life, been *herself*, a sometime graduate student in art history, a part-time assistant in children's book publishing, a lover, a mother. She had been herself reflected in familiar form by her friends and her employments, webbed by phone calls from her parents and three brothers in their scattered states, bound by the daily rituals of the doormen and the grocery store, by her daily exchanges with the local bag lady who squatted next to her bulging shopping cart, by all the little ties and lines that fetter, and constitute, a life.

Without these, with instead the rhythms of the artificial domain reverberating around her, she would become something else, something unimagined: what Chateau Deeds required: the lady of the house.

Because, as Alice Armstrong would soon discover, and as the family's newly elevated circumstances would endorse, a manor of the English style – however reduced in scale, however far from Olde England – could not run itself. There were, to begin with, the retainers, those that Lady Maureen had left behind, chief among them Davy Jones. His continued employment was a clause of the lease: his mistress wished to retrieve the gardens as she had abandoned them, for their coloured beds and statuary to be tended in her absence. Under Davy's salty supervision, on more intermittent visits, there were the window washers (once a month), the gutterers (twice a year), and the handyman, Davy's nephew Nigel, when occasion demanded it.

Lady Maureen had let her housekeeper go – Mrs Spirelli had been near retirement anyway, and grateful for an excuse to return to her flat near Bondi Beach – and so there was, at first, nobody besides Alice herself to wax the parquet and dust the shepherdesses, to water the ferns in the conservatory and polish the brass lion's-head knockers on the double-fronted door. Let alone the everyday tasks of washing and ironing, of cleaning toilets and beating the rugs, of preparing the meals and mopping the linoleum in the cavernous kitchen. Alice tried to teach the girls to make their beds and tidy their toys, but they could not understand the point of making a bed which you were only, then, to unmake again that evening; and enraptured by the acreage of space allotted to them alone, Martha and Sadie yearned fully to inhabit it, strewing dolls and Lego sets and their father's old toy soldiers all across the playroom's painted floorboards.

"Teddy." One night at supper, after the girls were in bed, Alice interrupted one of her husband's less entertaining office anecdotes, which involved imitating an Australian accent – something he did not yet do particularly well. "I think I need some help here. The house is too damn big."

"No problem, sweetie. Find someone, and hire her." Teddy's acquiescence was immediate and indifferent: they were flush, after all, and he was in the middle of his story.

Thus began Alice's marathon search for a day girl. She asked several of the neighbours – stout and doughty matrons, whose help had been with them for years – to no avail. She asked a couple of her daughters' schoolmates' mothers, and there found some assistance, but all the women they suggested lived too far away, or were already too busy, or came to see the house and shook their heads regretfully at its grandiosity, saying, "It's too much for me, madam, even at three days a week."

Finally, having resisted the scrawled cards posted at the supermarket door, Alice gave in to one, carefully and childishly printed, that she discovered on the bulletin board at the local public library (a superior source, she told herself, as it attracted a literate clientele). And so Miss Bliss, the first of the hired help, came to Chateau Deeds.

Miss Bliss was the first visitor to wield the lion's-head knockers (there was in fact a doorbell to the right of the front door, which everyone else seemed to locate without difficulty). Alice Armstrong was above, in her bathroom, at the time, and upon hearing the resounding boom in the hall below at first thought that the marble bust ("*après* Rodin") had fallen from its pedestal at the foot of the stairs. When she opened the door to her prospective employee, she was surprised to see before her a person who looked less like a cleaner than like a child escaped from a fairy-tale. Miss Bliss could not have been older than eighteen. Bird-boned, she was little over five feet tall, with white-blonde hair that fell loose almost to her waist, restrained only by rather promi-nent ears. Her skin was of skim milk pallor, and her eyes, between their bleached lashes, were a watery blue, rimmed with red.

"I'm here about the job," the girl explained, in a voice hardly above a whisper. "I'm Miss Bliss."

"Of course you are," said Alice, thinking how disconnected from her name the anxious girl appeared. "Come in."

As Alice showed her charge around the house, Miss Bliss did little more than nod, occasionally, and widen her rabbit eyes. Sometimes her tiny pink tongue slipped out between her lips and hovered for a second, as if taking the air, but she remained remarkably silent. In and out of the rooms they went, up and down the echoing halls. In the huge kitchen, Miss Bliss steadied herself with both hands at the counter, as if overwhelmed by the dull gleam of the appliances and the multitude of cabinets. There, she finally spoke again: "There's two fridges," she observed.

"I know," agreed Alice. "Isn't it odd? I think the owners must have entertained a lot."

Miss Bliss looked at the floor, and sighed.

"Have you done this kind of work before?" asked Alice.

"Some," said Miss Bliss uncertainly.

"Because, as you can see, it's quite a big house. I mean, there's a lot to keep up with."

"I need the job, madam. I can work hard."

"I'm sure you can," said Alice soothingly, although she was not sure at all.

It was agreed that Miss Bliss would work Mondays, Wednesdays and Fridays from nine-thirty to one pm, beginning the Monday following.

"Will you be all right for transportation?"

"Madam?"

"To get here – can you get here okay? Do you live nearby?"

"Not very. But I'll manage. I've got to."

"And you know, please don't call me 'madam'. I'm just plain old Alice. Okay?"

"Yes'm," said Miss Bliss. But she did not say "Alice", and she did not offer her own first name. To the Armstrongs, she would remain Miss Bliss forever.

This was in part because forever, at least insofar as it regarded the *presence* of Miss Bliss, was short-lived.

On Monday morning, nearer ten than nine-thirty, Alice answered Miss Bliss's pounding knock, and opened the door to discover on the threshold the girl – clad in jeans, as before, but with a faded flowered smock over her T-shirt, and with her hair caught back in a straggling plait – clutching to her side, with both pale hands, an immense Moses basket in which nestled a baby, only a couple of months old but as plump, ruddy and vigorous as its parent was wan.

"I hope you don't mind about Little Jim," whispered Miss Bliss, peering anxiously up at Alice.

"My mum couldn't have him today. But he won't be a bother, madam, I promise."

Startled but sympathetic, Alice beckoned them in. "I'll leave you to it,' she said. "I'm just taking care of some letters. I'll be upstairs. Maybe you could do the ground floor today, and then we'll worry about the rest next time." So saying, she withdrew. Never having had hired help, it did not occur to Alice that such a person might need direction or instruction, particularly if they had previously done little domestic work.

For half an hour, at her desk (it was Lady Maureen's of course) in the study next to her bedroom, Alice heard no sounds at all. She wondered if Miss Bliss was dusting, or whether she had, instead, slipped into the kitchen to fix herself a snack – she looked, poor girl, so starved. Curious, Alice wanted to check, if only to be sure the girl was not sliding Lady M's silver cutlery into the basket alongside Little Jim. The idea that there was someone other than her family in the rooms with her distracted Alice; she felt she should at least *hear* the girl: in her silence, Miss Bliss seemed to spread, like an ether, and fill the house far more substantially than her tiny frame and invisible character might have suggested. Noise, Alice thought, would have placed and contained her; without it, she could be anywhere.

She was just resolving to venture downstairs on the pretext of offering coffee when Little Jim began to wail, a lusty, powerful, relentless wail with the rhythm of waves against the shore. Alice opened her door, and the cries grew louder, accompanied by barely audible clucks and soothing murmurs from Miss Bliss. Alice could tell they were in the foyer, just below. She stood at the top of the stairs and listened, wondering whether to call out, offer assistance, feeling for a moment as if she herself were the servant, new and uncertain of responsibilities. To combat this foolish anxiety she started, with a firm tread, down the marble steps.

"Everything okay there?" she asked, in her deepest voice, as she descended, and receiving no answer, proceeded all the way.

Miss Bliss was on her knees in the middle of the sea of black-and-white parquet, with Little Jim's basket before her and, looped around them, the cords and tubing of the old-fashioned vacuum cleaner which sat, like a blue-and-silver dachshund, an arm's length away upon its little feet, as if preparing to make a dash for the living-room door. Miss Bliss's white face was crimson with effort, and her smock and T-shirt were rucked up below her neck, revealing a pale and skimpy bosom. In her arms she heaved the screaming infant, whose gaping mouth she strove to direct towards one or other of her pink nipples. Alice's own mouth fell open.

"Sorry, madam, it's just, he's hungry, and I'm still trying – they say, the midwife said, it's better this way than a bottle —"

"Of course, of course." Alice recovered herself. "I'll be right upstairs then, if you need anything."

After Miss Bliss left at one, hauling the Moses basket beside her like her life's burden, Alice walked through the ground-floor rooms that the girl had supposedly cleaned. There were indeed the marks of the vacuum cleaner – and Alice had heard its roar, after Little Jim was again quiet – along the carpets, and the surfaces appeared to have been at least cursorily dusted. But the cushions in the drawing room remained unpuffed, and the breakfast dishes unwashed in the sink, and even as she surveyed these latter, Alice realized that her sandals were crunching on an unswept hoard of crumbs upon the kitchen floor.

Never mind, she told herself. It's a beginning. The girl will learn. We'll both learn.

That evening she recounted the story of her morning to her family. Martha and Sadie were delighted at the idea of a baby – "Can they come at the weekend, Mom?" asked Martha, whose vowels were already broadening into an Australian twang. "Can we get to see him?" – and Teddy chuckled at the image of the girl breastfeeding in the hall – "Like a Madonna, eh? Miss Blissful Madonna. You should've brought her a pillow or something, Al. She must've been damned uncomfortable."

"I didn't think of it, right at that moment, weirdly enough."

"Can we see her feed him?" asked Martha. "Can we feed the baby too?"

"Maybe someday," said her mother. "But not just yet."

On the Wednesday, however, Alice Armstrong, who had planned to go to the supermarket, waited at Chateau Deeds all morning in vain expectation of Miss Bliss's arrival. She thought that the girl might at least have telephoned. She had surmised that the young mother was much alone with the baby, and knew from experience how suddenly a crisis might evolve – diarrhoea, a sudden temperature, a worrying excess of vomit – and she sought to be understanding. But it was strange that Miss Bliss did not call on Wednesday night, nor on Thursday, not least because she was not to have been paid until Friday afternoon; and when Friday noon came and went with no sign, Alice Armstrong gave the girl up for lost.

Alice retrieved the slip of paper with Miss Bliss's phone number from her wallet, but she only briefly considered calling. The round and careful numbers, deeply imprinted on the page, brought to mind the girl's pink tongue, emerging upon her lip in deep concentration; and the memory of the poor girl, so oppressed and bedraggled, so disheartened Alice that she wadded the slip into a firm pellet, and threw it away.

It took several weeks of concentrated effort to find Africa. She came to them as the indirect result of a conversation with Sadie's kindergarten teacher, Miss Luddy, a beaky spinster with bottle-bottom glasses and a distinct tremor of the hands. Miss Luddy mentioned Asia, the West Indian woman who cleaned the elementary-school classrooms in the evenings; and Asia, it transpired, was one of three sisters, along with America and Africa. All worked as cleaners, America of corporate offices downtown (she and Asia had children of their own and went to work only once their husbands had come home), and Africa of houses.

Alice first met Africa, then, in the company of Asia, both blousy women with deep voices who laughed frequently and at the same pitch. Africa was very tall, as tall as Teddy, with skin the rich colour of milk chocolate, glossy and smooth; Asia was shorter, and so seemed stout, and her colouring was fairer, her eyes green and the bridge of her nose dotted with freckles. To Alice, the sisters with their generous, calm manner were reassuring, and when Africa agreed to come to Chateau Deeds (although only twice a week, as that was all her schedule would permit), and when she declared, upon meeting Martha and Sadie, that they were "dear little girls, so smart in their uniforms, reminds me of back home", in far-off St Kitts, Alice felt the prickle of grateful tears behind her eyes.

There ensued five splendid months for the Armstrong household. Africa not only came on time, without fail, and took efficient charge of the running of the house, she also taught Alice how to cook special recipes – a spicy veal stew, a particular buttery cake with fruit compote – and sat, after her work was done, chatting with her employer about her nieces and nephews, about barbecues in the park with Asia and America, about her two brothers-in-law (one villainous and short-tempered, the other placid but unsuccessful in employment). She recounted amusing anecdotes about her boyfriend, a Ukrainian émigré in his forties who built doll's-house furniture and always wanted to take her camping: "Picture me in the wilderness? Like I could stand the crawlies and the snakes. No way!" But when Alice came across a fat and hairy huntsman, the size of a butter plate, basking in the sun in the conservatory, and screamed in terror, Africa did not balk: she fetched the broom, whisked him from his perch, and promptly stomped upon him, crushing his large body under her foot but leaving his legs, themselves large, wiggling on either side of her shoe. "Don't mind, Alice," she said. "He don't bite. He just likes the warm air. Just like you and me. In the wrong place at the wrong time, that's all. Comes to all of us."

Africa got on famously with the taciturn gardener, Davy Jones, invited him into the house for coffee and pried from him stories of his dead wife and rebellious daughter, of his hopes for his nephew Nigel, whom he wanted to be an electrician with a proper diploma. In the manner of an excellent hostess, she brought Alice and Davy together in her kitchen over tea and digestives, and forced them to overcome their reserve, so that long after she was gone, Davy would open conversations with his temporary mistress with the query, "Any news of Africa?"

She appreciated Davy's garden – the roses especially – and would clip one or two of the most richly scented ones and slip them, in a bud vase, by Alice's side of the bed. She brought chocolate treats for the girls, whom she rarely saw, and once a pair of glow-in-the-dark yo-yos, one yellow, one green, that Martha and Sadie squabbled over for a week.

Alice felt that in Africa she had found her first Australian friend, although of course Africa was no more Australian than Alice herself, so when Alice told Teddy, she amused her buoyant husband no end. She looked forward all week to Mondays and Wednesdays, saved stories about the girls and their adventures to tell her employee, bought specially the slices of jellied tongue that Africa savoured for her lunch.

But the day came when, abruptly, the idyll ended. Africa arrived at the house unsmiling, and set about her work with solemn determination. Not till lunchtime did she explain her gloom, seated at the grey formica kitchen table with her head in her hands.

"Oh, Alice love, I'm sorry, but I've got to go away. Been crying about it all yesterday, and Sergei, he doesn't want to accept it. But it comes to all of us, isn't that the Lord's truth?"

The fact was, Asia, America and Africa's widowed mother Honoria had suffered a stroke, back in St Kitt's, the previous Friday. She was in hospital, couldn't move her right side, and could only mumble: the doctors weren't sure how much, if any, of her former mobility would return, and she needed a daughter beside her, at once, and possibly for a long time. Asia and America had children of their own; only Africa was free to go at a moment's notice, and the three sisters together had come up with enough money for the plane ticket.

Alice cried as she heard Africa's story, and welcomed the tall woman's embrace; but she felt ashamed. She wasn't really crying for Africa, or for Africa's sisters or their mother, nor even, truth be told, for bewildered Sergei, who called Africa "my queen" and had begged her not to leave. Alice was crying chiefly out of selfishness, at the prospect of losing her companion. But she didn't reveal this secret, because she wanted Africa to think her compassionate; and she called Teddy at work and got permission to write Africa a fat cheque, a month's wages, so then it was the other woman's turn to shed tears. On Wednesday, Africa did not come to Chateau Deeds, and on Thursday she flew out – to Hawaii, then Los Angeles, then Miami, then on, at last, to St Kitts, with no real certainty of what she would find.

It was some time before the Armstrongs tried again to find a housekeeper. Teddy's job was consuming, and he was good at it, well liked by colleagues. It had become clear that his prominence in the bank conferred upon Alice certain professional responsibilities of her own. She was, little as she enjoyed it at first, participating in ladies' lunches. (The Australian women, all wives like herself, seemed somehow older, and stiffer, than she. "Christ, Teddy," she complained to her husband, "Ariel Boote-Smith turned up wearing a hat and white lace gloves! Like something out of *Brideshead*! What kind of world is this?") In time she began to organize lunches as well. She met, too, with other mothers from the girls' school, and through them found herself roped into committees – for the annual school benefit auction, for the charity drive at the local spastic children's home. Her long, empty days alone in Chateau Deeds were no more.

Alice found she barely had time to deposit the girls at school, and could never be certain of picking them up on time. Once, she was close to half an hour late (she'd been shopping at Grace Bros with Ariel Boote-Smith, choosing presents for the upcoming office Christmas party, to be held – where else? – at Chateau Deeds), and found Martha fiercely clutching little Sadie who, dissolved in tears, was convinced that their mother had plunged headfirst down the marble staircase and lay dead and undiscovered in a crimson pool on the front hall parquet. Martha, by then seven, was too brave herself to have wept, and too young yet to rail openly at her mother, but there was bitter accusation in her voice when she informed Alice, "We thought you must be dead. At least!" and Alice imagined she heard, implicitly, "and we wish you were!"

So it was on the advice, again, of a faintly disapproving Miss Luddy, that Gary came into their lives. Gary was the feckless son of the school's Deputy Principal, a long-haired blond boy of twenty or so who had never finished high school, had worked odd jobs in Queensland, and had lately returned to his parents' hearth short of luck and money. At his mother's instigation, he had at last created for himself a niche – as a chauffeur of smaller schoolgirls in an independent car pool, and he shuttled some half a dozen charges to and from the school in Vaucluse. He drove a large station wagon, blue with fake wood trim, and only slightly dented, in which he assembled his giggling cargo: one in front, alongside him, four in the back seat, and a couple stuffed higgledy-piggledy in the very back, on a piece of tatty carpet, where they rolled and pinched each other among the piled school cases.

Gary, with his rangy limbs and unkempt clothes, was not especially presentable – even less so when he tried to tidy up and pulled his hair off his face with an elastic: this style seemed somehow to accentuate his chipped front tooth, and lent him a frankly louche air – but Alice took heart from the confidence of the other mothers, and from the fact of his elevated parentage. He was always prompt and courteous, and her girls, pleased that he allowed them to sing in the car whereas their mother did not, seemed quite prepared to accept the new routine.

In the same week as Gary took Chateau Deeds into his rounds, Alice hired a caterer for the upcoming Christmas party. At the recommendation of Ariel Boote-Smith (who, despite her hat and gloves, proved fairly amusing, not least in her sharp-tongued commentary upon the other bankers' wives), Alice turned to Madame Poliakoff, a tiny, chic Russian lady of her own age who wore as many rings as she had fingers and conducted her kitchen like an orchestra from the precarious perch of three-inch heels. Madame Poliakoff ("Sounds like a clairvoyant, not a cook!" mused Teddy) employed in turn an array of waiters, all of them neat and demure girls from good families and enrolled in expensive cooking courses. She drove a white van upon the side of which, in curly purple script, her name appeared, with the motto *Delicious foods, savoury and sweet, for all occasions*, and beneath that, in smaller print, *No event too big or too small.*

The Christmas party – the Armstrongs' first Australian Christmas – would be a great success. The early summer was hot. The afternoons brought not too blasting a heat, but a glorious, strong sun, which seemed to Alice like a blessing on the land. She found it disconcerting, but not unpleasant, to celebrate the invernal holiday in estival surroundings. Alice procured a ten-foot artificial tree for the conservatory, and swaddled its plastic trunk with white cotton batting intended to imitate snow. Martha and Sadie spent an afternoon winding garlands and tinsel around the scratchy plastic branches and balancing glittering glass baubles from their ends. Teddy saw to the lights, a twinkling cascade of blue and green, and Alice climbed the ladder to crown the tree with the bisque angel they had brought, packed among their winter clothes, all the way from New York.

The party took place on the twentieth of December, in the afternoon. On the nineteenth, Ariel Boote-Smith came by and she and Alice locked themselves in the library with rolls of gaudy paper and gifts for each and every one of the bank's children: board games and jigsaw puzzles, Barbie dolls and magic sets, cap guns, and, for an eight-year-old budding zoologist whose mother was the office manager, a plastic bottle with small holes pierced in its lid, sold as a "bug catcher". They wrapped and chatted and gossiped, and Alice felt particularly the absence of Africa when she had to interrupt their retreat, first to go make the tea and lay out a plate of biscuits for her guest, and again when she felt obliged to check on the girls, home for the holidays, quietly drawing and colouring on huge squares of pulpy paper laid out on the playroom floor.

"It's just such a big house," she complained to Ariel upon her return, "that it's hard to take care of everything. The girls could be wreaking all kinds of havoc upstairs and I'd never know – we wouldn't even hear them."

"You've got a service flat, haven't you?" asked Ariel, wrinkling her long nose slightly in an expression that might have been envy and might have been disdain. "I mean, Lady Deeds had this place built for servants. You've got responsibilities now, with Ted's job, and you want to be an asset to him, don't you?"

"Of course I do." Alice patted anxiously at her hair. "But I don't see —"

"You need a live-in, is what I'm saying. You can't do *your* job unless you have someone proper to do *that* job. No two ways around it. You need a live-in."

"Maybe. I don't know, I —"

"We'd have one ourselves if Jack hadn't insisted on the house being completely open-plan, totally unsuited to live-in help. And of course, by now the boys are old enough to take care of themselves, or just about. But *here,* well . . . I frankly don't know how you manage. I'd *insist,* if I were you."

Alice shrugged, fiddled with a piece of Scotch tape. She was wrapping a set of plastic jewellery for Ted's secretary's youngest, Polly.

"You really should raise it with him, Alice. Men don't have a clue. He probably has no idea how long it takes to dust that parlour properly, let alone the rest of it – and those girls are a handful all right."

Even as Ariel Boote-Smith spoke, the two women could hear a curious repetitive thudding from the hall. Alice went to investigate and found that her daughters were taking turns sliding, bumpety-bump, down the marble staircase on a rush beach mat nicked from the linen cupboard.

"It's like a magic carpet, Mummy. It's the best," cried Martha, her round cheeks red and her eyes wide. "It's the best fun."

"Just be careful, sweetheart. It would really hurt if you bumped your head."

"We won't. I'm very careful. And I make Sadie be careful too."

"And try to be quiet, okay? Mrs Boote-Smith and Mummy are working." Alice put a finger to her lips. She wondered if she should stop the girls, but it didn't seem fair: they were so gleeful, bouncing down the steps on their bottoms, that she almost envied them, and at least now they were within earshot.

"They're just playing," she told her companion. "I think they're all right."

Ariel pursed her lips, shook her head slightly, and bent further over the half-folded package in front of her.

On the morning of the party, Madame Poliakoff arrived so early that Teddy, in his shirt and boxer shorts, had to summon Alice from her ablutions.

"Al, that lady of yours is here," he called, and pointed from the window down to the drive, where Madame Poliakoff, in pink mules and a miniskirt, was emerging from her van.

"Shit," said Alice, trying at one and the same time to button her blouse and brush her hair. "I haven't cleaned up from breakfast yet. I don't suppose *you* could — I mean, if I go get the door, you could pop down the back stairs and just give the dishes a quick rinse —"

"I'm in my shorts here, Al," Teddy whined. "And besides, I promised the girls I'd be ready twenty minutes ago. They've been squawking since seven — 'The park, the park, let's go to the park!' *You're* the one who wanted them out of the house this morning."

"But Teddy —"

The doorbell rang, a long, insistent buzz. Teddy looked out the window again. "Davy's pulling in too, Al. He's got that boy in the car – what's his name?"

"Nigel. His name is Nigel. They're here to put up the tent on the side lawn. They're early. Maybe you could just go over it with them, you know, exactly *where,* so there isn't any mistake . . ."

But Teddy had slipped into the bathroom. She could see him lathering soap for his shave. "Nigel," he was muttering to his reflection in an imitation Australian accent. "G'day, Nigel. Howzit going, Nigel? This is me mate, Nigel . . ."

"Damn you, Teddy," Alice hissed under her breath as she made for the stairs. "Damn you to hell."

Alice led Madame Poliakoff to the side door, down the path alongside the garage, then between the walled garden and the kitchen side of the house, past the shed where Davy stored his tools. The gravel was unraked there, and Madame Poliakoff teetered like a tightrope walker on her heels, clucking her tongue.

"So, I can back up van to here?" she inquired, with a formidable rolling of her 'r's, indicating with a jewelled forefinger and tossing her coppery head. "It's okay. This van is only first trip. Later, I make two, three trips. Don't worry, there will be plenty to eat for your guests."

"I'm sure there will," agreed Alice brightly. She opened the side door and led Madame Poliakoff to her command post, where the caterer, who had been there twice before on elaborate reconnaissance missions, clapped her dainty hands together and sighed. "I love this kitchen. This is perfect kitchen for parties. Two of everything, just as we need it, so . . ." She paused, and peered at the jam-stained, butter-daubed breakfast dishes in their little pool of crumbs, frowned at the open box of Frosted Flakes, the uncapped bottle of milk. She seemed to wince. "In this warm weather," she advised, "is very important to put milk in refrigerator – otherwise, it's making at once yoghourt." She put the emphasis on the second syllable: "yo*ghourt*." Alice felt that this comment was really an oblique way of condemning the girls' artificially sweetened cereal, of expressing disapproval for a breakfast that did not consist of tiny glazed pastries and coffee made with steamed milk.

"Well," she countered brusquely, "I usually *do* put it away. But you caught us rather off guard, so early. The pantry, as you may recall, is this way; and if you need extra room for, I don't know, trays of canapés, or if your girls —"

"My waitresses," corrected Madame Poliakoff with an authoritative glint.

"Yes, well, if they need a place to change, or sit down, or whatever, we've cleared the coat room, here, and —"

"Mrs Armstrong?" Davy Jones, in his tweed flat cap and flannel shirt in spite of the heat, loomed wiry but inescapable at the side door. Nigel, tall, plump and egg-headed, with a rash of spots that disappeared in a trail inside the neck of his tattered T-shirt (advertising Castlemaine XXXX), hovered outside, kicking at the gravel.

"Yes Davy?"

"Excuse me, but we need to get on with the tent."

"Of course you do. Of course. Davy, Madame Poliakoff. This is Mr Jones, our gardener."

The two did not shake hands. Madame Poliakoff inclined her head in a bird-like gesture, while Davy eyed the caterer's skirt and shoes and then gazed downwards.

"I'll let you set up, then, or get started," Alice said to the caterer. "I'll be right back. We'll just be on the side lawn if you need me." So saying, Alice hustled Davy out the door, pushed past Nigel and headed, with great purpose, back to the sunlit drive. She could hear Madame Poliakoff's heels crunching on the gravel behind them in an uneven rhythm.

"Madame," came the Russian's voice. "About the milk, so? I put in refrigerator, and —"

"Please don't worry about our breakfast things. I'll get to them as soon as I can. They surely aren't so much in the way, for ten minutes?" Alice smiled, to soften her irritation, but Madame Poliakoff did not. She reminded Alice, in that moment, of Ariel Boote-Smith – who had, now that Alice thought of it, recommended the woman.

As Alice, Davy and Nigel tramped under the portico, she saw her husband standing goofily at the front door in his turquoise Hawaiian swimming trunks, three large towels tucked under his arm, a red plastic pail in his hand, and, on top of his rusty curls, a crumpled white hat with a floppy brim.

"Hey, Davy, Nigel! Girls changed their minds," he said to Alice. "We're just headed down the road to the beach, okay?"

Alice did not deign to respond.

"We'll be back by noon." Teddy's voice floated across the hedge. "Be all cleaned up by two, ready for the big event."

Davy lit a cigarette and tucked it into the corner of his mouth. "That lady foreign?" he asked.

"Russian, yes. She's a very good caterer."

He nodded. "Shame about Africa, eh?"

"Right about now, it seems like a pretty terrible shame, Davy, it's true. But she wasn't a caterer, anyway."

"S'pose not," said Davy. "The roses've got aphids again, in spite of us. I'll spray 'em on Monday."

"Monday's Christmas Day," said Alice.

"All the same."

"Got any plans for the holiday then, Nigel?"

The youth, startled, opened his piggy eyes wide.

"We'll all be round my sister's," said Davy. "Out by Randwick."

"Going to the races, then?"

"No races at Christmas. Maybe Boxing Day," mumbled Nigel. "But Mum doesn't like it."

"Course she don't," sneered Davy. "Smart boy like you throwing away good money on the nags."

"But you said —" began Nigel.

"Nuff, Nige. Let's get on with the tent." He looked at Alice. "Where do you want 'er?"

She strode across the grass to the conservatory steps, a gracious semicircle of pink stone spreading like ripples out from the house. "The tree's in there," she said, "so I thought right outside, just here. It's the logical place."

"Lady Deeds always had the tent over by the roses." Davy indicated a stretch of lawn nearer the front of the house. "So the guests would come right in, through the hedge, and have a drink there."

"Ye-es," said Alice, "but for the Christmas tree, you see —"

"Ground ain't level here," Davy continued. "See how it goes, sloping off already?"

"But I thought —"

"We're not experts," he insisted, bullish now, reddening beneath his cap. "You'd need different-sized poles for the sloping ground, wouldn't you?"

"Else the tent might topple over," agreed Nigel with a smirk. "With all the guests inside."

Alice was quiet for a moment.

"Pardon me saying so," said Davy, pushing his cap back on his forehead, "but Lady Deeds built the house, as it were. And the gardens. She knew it best – *knows* it best. That spot over there – it's what's best for a party."

"I don't want a tent there. I want it here." Alice's voice was rising of its own accord, and she heard it as if from far away.

"As you like, Miz Armstrong. But we're not expert tent men."

"It could fall over," repeated Nigel, biting his lip now and scratching the rash on his neck.

"I just wouldn't advise it," said his uncle. "For that spot, you should've hired experts."

"But if you turned it this way –" Alice tried to show them what she had intended. "It's rectangular, so it would, if it ran alongside the house rather than perpendicular —"

"Still too wide, I'm afraid. Believe me."

Davy and Nigel looked at each other – Alice saw it – and then Nigel gaped up at the lone cumulus cloud trailing across the sky, while his uncle resumed his habitual scrutiny of the ground.

"This is ridiculous," Alice said. "I can't believe —"

"I've been here seventeen years last September, madam, and I've known a lot of parties. Lady Deeds is very particular —"

"Yes. Well." Alice crossed her arms over her chest and glared out over the neighbours' roofs towards the water. She imagined her husband and daughters frolicking on the shore, only a few hundred yards away. She could smell the salt on the air. She licked a dot of sweat from her lip, and listened to the sound of Madame Poliakoff revving her van in preparation for the next trip, the next load of trays. Soon the truck from the liquor store would arrive, and the florist with the Christmas wreaths – alternating banksias and waratahs, the man had promised. "A real Aussie display."

"So you won't do it," she said at last.

"Not a matter of won't, Mrs Armstrong. Don't get me wrong. Matter of can't, that's all. Experts, you need."

Seventeen years doesn't make you an expert except when you want to be, thought Alice, wondering only vaguely how nakedly her loathing shone upon her face. "Well, that's that, then," she said. "We'll do without the tent."

"I'm sorry?"

"It's a perfect day, no risk of rain; we'll do without the tent."

"Gets very hot in the sun," said Nigel.

Alice glared at the boy. "Too bad," she said. "The faint-hearted can stay inside. We'll do without the tent. I'd rather not have it than see it floating off there in the middle of nowhere like a runaway balloon."

"Looks lovely by the roses," said Davy, but softly, almost under his breath.

"Thanks for your time, guys. I'll make sure Teddy – Mr Armstrong – pays you just the same. But no tent."

"It's a crying shame," said Davy.

"I couldn't agree with you more. But no tent."

When Alice retreated, wrathful, to her temporarily unpeopled kitchen, she was initially restored by the sight of Madame Poliakoff's elegant trays: stuffed cherry tomatoes and zucchini flowers, little boats of miniature eggplant, sculpted cantaloupes festooned with wee prosciutto banners, nasturtiums elaborately arranged around militarily arrayed puff pastries, bite-sized, in which nestled crab salad or tiny shrimp in sauce or a festive mix of red and green pepper diced very finely. These were only the cold canapés, kept from the air by clear plastic held aloft by toothpicks (just like the tent, thought Alice, of which Davy and Nigel had so obstinately deprived her), and brightened and ordered by green leaves and silver foil. She thought that Madame Poliakoff, at least, was on her side, to have created such splendour, but then she caught sight of the breakfast dishes, sparkling on the drainboard in, as Alice took it, victorious reproach, and she was flooded with a new wave of rage and helplessness that prompted her to curse her husband again.

In her mind's eye, she saw him on the front doorstep in his absurd trunks and hat, his ginger-haired legs pale and faintly bandy above his thongs – on this day of all days – grinning his stupid grin. "Damn you, Teddy," she said aloud. "Damn you to hell."

None of the guests, however, once they arrived, had the slightest suspicion about the morning's disasters (none, that is, except Ariel Boote-Smith, who took Alice aside early on and whispered, "Something happen to the tent, dear? I don't see the tent." To which Alice, without missing a beat, replied, "With this beautiful weather? I decided it would just be in the way.") The circular drive was fast packed with cars, as were the two roads outside the walls. The bankers and their families, the secretaries and theirs, the computer programmers and the cleaners and the office juniors all streamed in through the gates as if to a village fete, giggled dutifully at the holly branch placed in Pan's arms in the middle of the trickling fountain, and accepted, from one or other of Madame Poliakoff's demure, black-and-white-clad waitresses (who were posted, at the *grande dame*'s insistence, just as Davy had predicted, right inside the hedge on the side lawn, by the roses), a glass of champagne or a diabolo menthe or a bright grenadine cocktail – a Shirley Temple, in truth, served either with or without gin – these last two beverages served for the occasion on account of their Christmas colours.

Martha and Sadie, in their flowered party dresses with puffed sleeves and smocking, quickly became ringleaders – "Hostesses in the making," jested one guest, a lean and leathery colleague of Teddy's in a flowered shirt of his own – of the younger children, tearing around the gardens, into the walled enclosure and the aviary and back again, making up elaborate games of cowboys and Indians, and airplanes and horses, in which, Martha bossily insisted, each child had a preordained and immutable role, while the older ones hovered awkwardly beside their parents, stiff in skirts or pressed trousers, casting surreptitious glances at their peers. Teddy was a genial and welcoming boss, Alice could see, handsome in his white, open-necked shirt, burnt slightly by the morning's sun, his caterpillar eyebrows roving rapidly through exaggerated expressions of delight and surprise. He had the politician's habit, when introduced to spouses of either gender, of clasping their proffered hand between both of his own and establishing apparently infinite eye contact. The women, in particular, were visibly charmed.

Alice, too, smiled broadly and constantly, laughed gaily, chattered with her guests regardless of age and station. Only once did she slip out to the kitchen, to visit Madame Poliakoff,

Napoleonic in her domain; but the Russian clearly neither needed nor wanted direction, and would brook no interruption.

"Now, so, you leave practical matters for my team, yes? Go, be hostess, have no cares, enjoy beautiful party. Make guests happy," she insisted, her rings clicking as she shooed Alice away.

Thus relieved of responsibility, Alice returned to the garden and allowed herself to forget about everything but the entertainment of her visitors, an unburdening so novel that she was prompted to concede to Teddy, that night in bed, all irritation of the morning long forgotten, "That Poliakoff woman is a miracle! Did you see the kitchen when they were done? Cleaner than it's ever been. I've never enjoyed one of our own parties before."

"That's great, Al. Because we really should be doing more of it – giving parties, I mean. Now that you've found her —"

Alice laughed. "We can have a party every evening?"

Teddy made a mock grimace. "Maybe once a week would be enough, don't you think?"

"I don't know, dear. Martha and Sadie asked for every day."

The highlight of the party had been the opening of the children's presents. Flushed by the sun and the abundant cocktails, the adults had assembled with their offspring in the conservatory around five, as the sky outside began to pale. Martha and Sadie, proud and proprietorial of their glimmering tree, had played Santa, distributing the parcels among their newfound friends and, more shyly, to the few older children. The budding zoologist had been particularly thrilled by her bug catcher, but in truth almost every gift had been a success, with the possible exception of a handful of novels and history books purchased for the teenagers. All the parents had oohed and aahed in chorus at each unwrapping – and their enthusiasm had prompted the little ones to smile their hapless gap-toothed smiles, even when they were initially uncertain about their toys. Once or twice a mother had to bend over her puzzled boy or girl and say, "Look, darling, it's an airplane that you put together yourself. Isn't it *lovely*?" And, pointing at the image on the box, "See the stickers for the wings? See the little pilot in his cockpit? Now isn't that a beautiful present? Say thank you, dear. Say thank you."

Everyone did say thank you, adults and children alike, many times; and as Alice and Teddy stood under the portico at dusk, shaking hands, dispensing kisses, waving at the departing crowd, Alice felt a blooming warmth in her chest and across her cheeks, a sensation of pleasure that she could not easily have expressed, but if she had tried, she would have said its origins were aristocratic: the pleasure came of giving pleasure, as if it were an endlessly bountiful commodity, to so many who seemed, because of it, to be grateful, to look up to her, even to envy. It was the delight of the mistress of the manor, the reward of Lady Deeds.

Thus began the era of parties.

For Sadie's fifth birthday, in February, Alice organized an elaborate costume celebration and rented tiny dresses for the girls in the style of Marie Antoinette, complete with miniature powdered wigs. There was a parade around the drive of the children in their disguises, and a competition for the best costume, judged by Madame Poliakoff (who had made a three-tier chocolate cake in the shape of the number five in honour of the occasion). Martha and Sadie's dresses, as befitted the daughters of so grand a household, were noticeably finer than the ensembles of the other girls and boys; but they had been warned beforehand, as indeed had Madame Poliakoff, that as hostesses they could under no circumstances be awarded the prize. It was given, in the event, to a little girl dressed as a thief, with a black stocking on her head and inky bristles penned along her jaw, who trailed, throughout the party, a black plastic garbage bag on which her mother had stuck the word *LOOT* in bright orange paper letters. Sadie was too young to appreciate her seigneurial obligations, although Martha did her best to explain them, and when her friends had departed the little girl wept at the injustice of seeing the finest costume – her own – go unrewarded.

The Amstrongs held four-course dinners, with three different wines, served by Madame Poliakoff's waitresses, on the Deeds silver plate, in the Deeds crystal. They had drinks parties on the lawn, or in the grand drawing room. They had a barbecue; they had brunches. They had fun.

But still, in spite of Madame Poliakoff's spectacular cleanliness, in spite of the fact that the dishes and glassware were immediately returned, as if by elves, to their places in the cupboards, and the ashtrays emptied, washed, and replaced on the side tables round about, still Alice would waken the morning after such events with leaden dread at the prospect of vacuuming and sweeping and puffing and dusting, low in the knowledge that without her efforts the entire downstairs would remain a mess. And, if Alice were to be honest with herself, she was coming to believe that such labour was beneath her. Ariel Boote-Smith's advice on the eve of the Christmas party – advice which her friend had since repeated more than once – haunted Alice, who struggled with the notion of a live-in housekeeper, so alien to her own upbringing and culture, but who finally, after counting the number of times in a month that they hired babysitters for the girls, determined that it was a matter not of whim but of necessity.

"Teddy darling," she said, one evening at her dressing table (whence the ghost of Lady Deeds had long since been banished), "Miss Dewar's coming in this evening for the third time this week." Miss Dewar, lean and wholly Scottish, a sixty-year-old maiden lady who drove a lavender

Volkswagen bug of impressive vintage, was the girls' favourite babysitter.

"Is that a lot, do you think?" asked Teddy, who was fussing with his black tie.

"Help me with this necklace, Teddy. I need to talk to you."

And while Teddy, all thumbs, struggled with the clasp of the antique pearl and ruby necklace he had given her on Valentine's Day (to Alice Armstrong, who had been used, in their American life, to receiving a Hallmark card or a box of drugstore candy; although that other life seemed so long ago as to be almost unreal), while he hovered behind her, his newly brushed breath warm and moist against her ear, she outlined her requirements for a housekeeper.

"That whole flat is sitting empty, Teddy —"

"'Flat', is it now? Speaking Strine? No 'apartments' anymore? Did Ariel prep you for this one?"

"Don't be silly. We're here and here it's called a flat. And the house was built for live-in help. You don't have any idea, I don't think, of how much I do."

"Sure, Al. Sure I do."

"And then all these babysitters! If we had a proper housekeeper, who lived here, that would be part of her job, you know?"

"It's kind of a weird idea, Al, that's all – some stranger living in your house with you. Don't you think?"

"No, I don't think. Teddy, believe me, I've given this *a lot* of thought. I've been thinking about it for months. You didn't even consider what it might mean for me when you went out and rented this monstrosity, did you?"

"You seem to like it okay. I'd say you'd taken to it like a duck to water, Al. Duck to water."

"Don't call me a duck, even for a joke." Alice had been teased by her brothers in childhood about the outward turn of her toes. "Just listen, for a change. I've been up to my ears, taking care of this bloody place – and then there's Davy! I mean, really – Lady Deeds this, and Lady Deeds that . . . He's obstinacy incarnate." She powdered her nose vigorously. "But when Africa was here, he was quiet as a lamb – it's a question of respect, frankly, and because there's no housekeeper, no intermediary, he doesn't have any *respect* for me, he thinks *I'm* the housekeeper, for God's sake —"

"Al, Al baby — whatever you want."

"He comes to the kitchen door, I'm up to my elbows in dishwater; he comes to the front door and I'm on my knees swabbing the damned parquet. He looks in the window, and —"

"Al." Teddy spoke more loudly. He looked like a gambler in his dinner jacket, but his face, eyebrows aloft, was half amused, half pained. "Al, take it easy. You can do whatever you want. We can afford it, for now at least. Whatever you want. Now put on your shoes and let's go kiss the kids goodnight. We're half an hour late already. Chop, chop."

Even with Teddy's permission, Alice took some time to organize herself. She had to clean up the maid's flat, for starters, which had sat empty, growing cobwebs, for a year. Lady Deeds, clearly with the good cheer of her staff in mind, and perhaps under the unfortunate sway of 1960s aesthetics, had selected, as a decoration theme, the sunflowers of Van Gogh. The studio's walls were accordingly yellow, with a rather mustardy tinge, and the doors and trim orange. The drapes and double bedspread featured the artist's flowers, over and over again, like an insistent exclamation, so that the uniform chocolate synthetic of the sofa and armchair, slightly shimmery, slightly plush, came almost as a relief to the over-exercised eye. The floor was of painted boards, as in the girls' playroom, scattered with knotted rugs of red, ochre and brown. The room was a decent size, with a telephone, a large television, a separate bathroom and a kitchenette. In the back of the kitchenette cupboard, behind the odd assortment of the Deeds' chipped and discarded china, Alice discovered a collection of miniature alcohol bottles of the kind served on airplanes, all of them empty.

"Guess Mrs Spirelli liked her tipple," she observed to her daughters, who ran in and out, still in their school uniforms, while she conducted her inspection; but neither of the children knew what she meant.

Cleaning and airing the little flat depressed Alice: she could not put her finger on the origin of her gloom, whether it was to do with the unmistakable imprint of her imperious predecessor, or with the sad little reminders of Mrs Spirelli, but suddenly, for the first time in months, Alice felt assailed by the arbitrariness, the strange irrelevance, of her Australian existence. Bent over the tub (ochre also) in the little bathroom, the mingled scents of must and Ajax in her nostrils, she marvelled that she, Alice Armstrong, thirty-seven years old, of Buffalo, New York, should find herself in this position. It was as if she had awakened after a drugged sleep to unfamiliar surroundings, as if some irretrievable portion of her life had been stolen from her. She felt her heart palpitating, ferocious in her breast, and almost panicked. How do I get out of here? she thought. How do I get back to myself? Then, like the soothing doctor, anaesthetic in hand, another voice quieted the first. What are you thinking, you goose? it clucked. This is your life, and where you belong – your husband at work and your daughters playing nearby. You, yourself, are right here, right here.

That evening, when the children were in bed and Teddy was in the library poring over papers he had brought home from the office, Alice sat at her desk in her study, in the pool of the green glass lamp, and began a letter to her mother. She wanted to try to explain this feeling, which had subsided but which lingered still around her like the smell of smoke; but she found she could not. Any words she could give to it sounded melodramatic, said either too much or not enough. Like smoke, the experience dissipated as she tried to contain it. After several false starts, Alice crumpled the pages and tossed them, capped her pen, and went to watch a police drama on television.

To find live-in help, Alice followed, of course, the instructions of Ariel Boote-Smith, who, although she had never had staff of that ilk in her own home, assured Alice that the procedures were intimately known to her through several of her closest friends. Alice put an advertisement in the classified section of the *Sydney Morning Herald*, vaunting the qualities of the service flat and mentioning that light childcare responsibilities were part of the post, in addition to traditional housekeeping. She offered *Room, board and small salary commensurate with experience*, and then sat back to wait.

*

She received fewer responses than she might have hoped – only eight – and of these, three were clearly unsuitable. A girl of nineteen applied, whose hand reminded Alice all too powerfully of the sorry Miss Bliss; and a matron of seventy with decades of experience in "the finest homes in New South Wales". "But a woman of seventy, taking out the garbage and dusting under the beds? I don't see it!" Alice said to Ariel, who wrinkled her nose in assent. And a man applied also, a man of her own age, who noted that he preferred to be called a butler but that he was eminently capable of any housekeeping duties she might require. Of him she observed to her friend, "Well, he might be quite all right, but somehow, the idea of leaving the girls at home with a *man* – you just never know, do you?"

"And you can't be too careful," agreed Ariel.

The remaining five candidates were all women in midlife with professional housekeeping experience and references, or at least the promise of them ("sterling references", insisted one, a lady by the name of Simone Funk). Alice was determined to interview them all, and figured that, were she still undecided after the interviews, she would offer, to the most promising prospects, a trial forty-eight hours: two nights in the service flat, two days of work, for which they would, naturally, be properly paid.

"You sure about this?" asked Teddy. "What if one of them got it into her head to slit all our throats?"

"Teddy, come off it – we're considering hiring any one of them *for good*. Women don't slit people's throats, anyway. Or not without just cause."

"Make sure you check their references, eh? I mean, properly. Check them."

"Just the way you do, Teddy, when you hire someone at the bank."

"I don't have to eat breakfast with the guys at the bank. I don't want some hag clacking her false teeth over the Weet-Bix, Al. Awful."

"She'll have her own flat, Teddy. She won't want to eat breakfast with you anymore than you want to eat breakfast with her."

"We'll see," said Teddy morosely. "We'll see."

Three of the women she decided immediately were unsuitable, for a variety of reasons – one too sexy, one woman had a high, piping voice that grated intolerably on Alice's ear, and the third just gave her an uneasy feeling. Which left only Muriel Leclerc and Simone Funk.

Muriel Leclerc was in her late forties, small, spry and unassuming. She spoke fairly good English, but Alice liked the idea that she might also speak to the girls in French. It seemed, moreover, impressively cultured, the idea of a French housekeeper. She didn't know anyone else who had one. The only drawback with Muriel Leclerc, who promised, on top of cleaning and babysitting, her skills as a cook, was Monsieur Leclerc – Hubert, her husband, a chauffeur by profession, if profession it was, but just then unemployed. Muriel Leclerc – Madame Leclerc, as Alice took pleasure in calling her, with her best undergraduate accent – explained her situation with dignity, and appropriate apologies, and asked that she nonetheless be given a chance. She held her hands together as if in prayer, and said, "You will see, Madame Armstrong, you will not be disappoint." ("Where did the 'ed' go?" Alice asked Teddy with a smile. "It seemed so cute, the disappearing 'ed'.") Alice capitulated, and agreed to a two-day trial.

"You must bring your husband, though. Monsieur Leclerc. Because if we were all to live together —"

"Yes, of course, *d'accord,* of course," said Madame Leclerc, with a servile bobbing of the head which both pleased and rather alarmed Alice.

And then, most uncomplicatedly, there was Simone Funk, she of the "sterling references", an Australian originally from Wagga Wagga, who had been married, once upon a time, to a German named Funk – "But he drank, love, and I couldn't be doing with that." There was something salty about Simone Funk – Mrs Funk – that pleased Alice immediately. She had a sense of humour, a ready smile which revealed slightly discoloured teeth. She was very brown, with prematurely white hair which she fluffed and styled as though it were blonde rather than white; and the veins stood up on the backs of her hands and up her forearms in a way that implied, to Alice, capability and hard work. She had not dressed up for her interview – "I thought it best for you to see me just as I am, so you could make up your mind more easily" – but wore clean blue jeans and a pressed white shirt. She looked as though she might have just come in from horseriding, or as though she might be about to set off on a hike: vigorous, untrammelled.

"I'm not much of a cook," she conceded, "but I can grill a steak and fix an omelette. And I love kids. I've worked with kids a lot." She smiled her toothy smile. "Seems they like me, too, by and large." She provided, from her handbag, a neatly folded piece of foolscap on which she had typed the names and telephone numbers of her four previous employers, dating back eleven years.

"I know some people think it's easiest to carry around letters, but I reckon you want to hear it from the horse's mouth."

"Very wise," agreed Alice.

"And seeing as I keep in touch with all of my old employers – even the Beckers, who, as you can see from the phone number, have moved back to Cologne – that's in Germany, in Europe – anyways, seeing as I keep in touch, it's easy to give out the telephone numbers. And they've all said they don't mind. They won't mind if you call them. And you can ask anything you like about me. Anything."

Mrs Funk – whom Alice would always call Mrs Funk to her face, although somehow, in her mind, the older woman was "Simone" – was more than happy to schedule her two-day trial over the weekend, the day after the Leclercs.

"I mean, we're looking at a round-the-clock position, aren't we? I know all too well what it's like. And you probably need someone with the girls for this very Saturday night. Am I right?"

Alice, unaccountably, blushed.

"Course I am. So you make that plan with your hubby for whatever it is you've got to do, and don't think twice about it. No worries, no fear, Simone Funk is staying here."

"I can get the regular sitter, you know, it's not a —"

"Wouldn't dream of it. It'd be part of my job, wouldn't it? So let's get started on the right foot. Like I said, I love kids. I love 'em."

After meeting Simone Funk – whose virtues she extolled to Teddy that evening – Alice was tempted to cancel the Leclercs altogether. "I just warmed to her right away," she told her husband. "And I *like* Madame Leclerc, but —"

"You haven't seen them work yet, Al. You're hiring a housekeeper, not a playmate. You've gotta see them at *work.*"

"But it's to live in, isn't it? And that makes the personality count for more , you said yourself —"

"And you said, quite rightly, that they'll have

their own place. With their own door – the kitchen door is their front door. It's not their conversational skills that count."

"I suppose you're right that we have to give them both a try, anyway, before we decide. It's only fair."

"It's only fair."

So the Leclercs came on the Wednesday morning, early, two small people with two small overnight bags. They came directly to the side door, and knocked, and when Alice opened she saw Madame in the foreground, in her blouse and skirt and stockings, and Monsieur lurking behind. Right away, Alice did not like the look of Hubert Leclerc. He was livid of skin, for one thing, and she suspected him of tempers or of alcoholism or of both; and he seemed to her somehow shifty, unwilling to meet her gaze, flinching under frank scrutiny.

That said, Madame Leclerc was a marvellous housekeeper. She zipped around Chateau Deeds as though its cleanliness were her long-awaited heart's desire. She finished the rooms on the ground floor by lunchtime (when Alice, taking a shortcut down the back stairs, could hear the television going in the flat, concrete proof of the idleness of Monsieur, and could smell, in the stairwell, the nutty seeping odour of his cigarettes), then not only prepared a lovely platter of salads and cheeses for Alice's noon meal (taking some, Alice noted, on a tray up to her husband, as though he were an invalid), but proceeded to bake a batch of shortbread biscuits for the girls' afternoon tea.

Alice was overwhelmed by how much Muriel Leclerc managed to pack into the two days – carpet beating and floor waxing and all manner of chores (the polishing of the damned Deeds silver among them) that Alice had been putting off for months. But she also felt there was something rather sinister about this, as though Madame Leclerc, so efficient, so deferential, were a performing seal, and her sullen husband, locked away with the Van Gogh sunflowers, his cigarettes and the television set, were the animal trainer from the circus. Alice imagined that when Madame Leclerc retreated to the flat, her husband goaded and browbeat her, setting her ever more complicated tasks ("Repair the vacuum cleaner!" she imagined him barking. "Turn all the mattresses in all of the bedrooms!") which she then felt obliged to try, at least, to carry out. No, for all the words of praise Teddy heaped on Madame Leclerc's lentil and sausage supper, Alice was not convinced.

"There's something wrong between them. As a couple, I mean. It's not a healthy dynamic. He's, I don't know, he carries a threat of violence, somehow. He —"

"Come on, Al, don't you think you're exaggerating a bit? The guy can't be taller than five foot five, and he probably weighs about a hundred and thirty pounds, if that."

"Yes, but she's tiny. Everything's relative, isn't it?"

Teddy shrugged. "She's a mighty good cook. And everything is spick-and-span all right – even *I* can tell the difference."

"But Sadie's afraid of him."

"What are you talking about?"

Alice was only embroidering a little: Sadie had in fact asked why the man's skin was such a funny colour and why he looked so grumpy. "His anger frightens her. She told me so."

Teddy sighed. "Well, that's that, then. Sayonara to these tasty meals, I guess. Let's hope there's nothing wrong with the other woman —"

"Mrs Funk."

"Yeah, her. Because otherwise we're back to square one."

"I think she's going to work out, Teddy. I just have a feeling."

"But you know, Al, if you get a bad vibe, or if she's incompetent – just let it go. We can look again, now or later. I mean, we've done perfectly fine so far —"

"Don't start, Teddy. Please."

Teddy, in defeat, merely shook his head slightly.

Simone Funk arrived on Saturday morning, not quite as promptly, it is true, as the Leclercs had done. She came to the front door, where she both rang the bell and swung the knockers. (Resourceful, thought Alice. Shows she's covering all the bases.) And when Martha, blue-eyed, solemn, opened upon the prospective housekeeper, Mrs Funk set down her suitcase, got down on one knee so that she was about the same height as Martha, and stuck out a hand.

"How do you do, Miss Armstrong? Now would you be Sadie, or Martha?"

"Martha," mumbled Martha.

"Well, you've no idea how pleased I am to meet *you*," said Mrs Funk. "I've heard all about you from your mum. Would you be in grade two, then?"

"Three," replied Martha, a trifle defensively.

"How stupid of me," said Mrs Funk, batting at her brow with the heel of her hand in mock recrimination. "I never was any good at school, though. Not like you, I bet. I bet you're good at school, aren't you?"

Martha thought for a moment, then nodded, gravely.

"Of course we are," said Alice Armstrong, emerging, hand outstretched, from the alcove from which she had been approvingly monitoring this scene. "Welcome to our home, Mrs Funk. We call it –" she tittered – "Chateau Deeds."

"Oh, right?" Mrs Funk looked around her, at the walls and up the sweeping staircase. "Why's that, then?"

"Just my husband being silly. After the owners, the people who built it – Sir Robert and Lady Deeds."

"Right. I see," said Mrs Funk, with a slightly puzzled air. "So it's not yours, then?"

"Heavens, no," said Alice. "I'd never have made such hideous decorating choices! Just wait till you see your flat — the flat where you'd live if you came. It's quite a sight."

Mrs Funk seemed hardly to be listening. She had wandered to the living-room door, where she stood surveying the fuss and clutter, the china shepherdesses. "So all of this stuff belongs to Lady whatever —"

"Deeds. Yes. Which is all the more reason why we're concerned to take good care of it. No, me, I'm not attached to *things*."

"Course you're not," agreed Mrs Funk with a sidelong smile, and a wink for little Martha who leaned, moon-eyed, against her mother's leg, watching the stranger.

"But it'd be very inconvenient to break any of the stuff in here, because one senses," Alice smiled a severe and disdainful smile, "that Lady Deeds *does* care, rather a lot, about these horrible knick-knacks."

"Some people are like that, aren't they?" commiserated Mrs Funk.

"Oh, it's all been inventoried," said Alice with a wave. "Every last bit of it. She cares an awful lot."

Mrs Funk's white hair shone in the shadowy hallway, like a halo. "Materialistic," she said. "Isn't that the right word? Some people are just materialistic by nature." She sighed, as if this deformation of character were a tragedy akin to limblessness, or blindness. "But what can you do?"

Mrs Funk made different use of her forty-eight hours than had Muriel Leclerc. To be sure, Madame Leclerc had left the house very clean, so that Mrs Funk would have been hard pressed to find as many impressive tasks to undertake as had her predecessor. And of course she didn't sit around idle: she did dishes, and laundry, and ironing (for which she had a particular knack), and she made the girls' beds without being asked, and she asked Alice, with calm confidence, about the usual housekeeping rituals and where everything was kept. She repeated that she wasn't much of a cook, but said she'd be happy to prepare the girls' school lunches and, if provided with a list, to do the grocery shopping. She spent time talking with each member of the Armstrong family, including Teddy, but she did so in such a way, Alice noted to Teddy, as to remain unobtrusive. When asked if she wanted to take her meals with them (of an evening, with the Leclercs, the question had not been mooted: Madame had scuttled upstairs with a tray to join her husband, whose English had been barely conversational and whose temperament obviously did not incline him to society), Mrs Funk had laughed and said, "We'll play it by ear, I reckon. I'll eat with the girls when you're out for the evening, but otherwise you'll want your privacy, I imagine, just as I'll most likely want mine. I've got the telly up in my flat, and it's been good enough company for me since I turfed out Mr Funk, some years ago now I must say."

Alice and Teddy went off to their soiree on Saturday evening with no misgivings: Mrs Funk was feeding the girls baked beans on toast and a fried egg, followed by rice pudding from a tin, and Martha and Sadie seemed quite satisfied with such fare. She promised to tuck them in by eight-thirty, and to read to them from the book Alice had underway, and she thought off her own bat to ask which lights, if any, should be left on in case they woke in the night.

"I always ask," she said, "because I was afraid of the dark myself as a girl. For the longest time. It's silly, really, but you've got to remember how kids are, don't you?"

"You certainly do, Mrs Funk," said Teddy with his politician's smile on, as he adjusted his jacket and jangled the car keys in his pocket. "Are we ready, hon? We're already late."

"We women," joked Mrs Funk, "we learn early to keep you fellows waiting. It's bred into us, isn't it, love? Have a lovely time now. And don't worry about a thing. I've got the phone number just in case, but I'm quite sure I won't need it. Ta-ta!"

"You see what I mean, don't you?" asked Alice in the car. "There's just something *right* about her."

"Well," said Teddy, "she does seem ideal. She's got Sadie and Martha eating out of her hand already. And she's made herself right at home."

"What's that supposed to mean?"

"Oh, I like her, Al. I like her. But I'd say she's pretty cocksure; she's pretty certain she's going to get the job."

"And she *is* going to get the job. So she's not wrong there."

"Do me a favour, Al? Make a couple of calls before you finalize the deal? Because she'll be living in the *house,* eh? With us, in the house."

"Of course I'm going to check her references. What do you take me for? Do I tell you how to run your office, Teddy? Do I?"

*

And on Monday morning, after Mrs Funk had withdrawn, her little suitcase in hand and her white hair glowing, then her brown arm reaching out of her red Austin Mini in a jolly wave, which she accompanied with a comical *paarp-paarp* on the car horn, Alice sat down with the typed sheet of foolscap and prepared to call Simone Funk's references. The house, after the weekend, seemed particularly, unpleasantly, silent; it seemed to Alice to require Mrs Funk, with or without her sterling references. But she had promised Teddy, and she did not want to disappoint him.

The number of the first family, a Mr and Mrs Holmes, now of Brisbane, had been disconnected. The second name on the list, Walenska, struck Alice as Polish. She had to gather her courage before dialling, as she imagined an interlocutor with an impenetrably thick accent, someone as clipped and imperious as Madame Poliakoff, who might dismiss Alice's high American singsong out of hand. She felt powerfully her lack of experience as a domestic employer, and retrieved her poise only by assuring herself that this was as much work as had been her position in publishing in New York, in which she had spent hours of each day on the phone with strangers, asking unexpected questions.

Her pep talk to herself was, however, in vain: the line rang hollowly at the other end. She let it trill, imagining the great caverns of the Walenska mansion, and a servant in a black-and-white uniform scurrying along intricate corridors towards a distant, lonely apparatus. Perhaps, she thought as she replaced the receiver in its cradle, after counting thirty-seven rings, the Walenska family was on an extended holiday in Europe, in a chateau in Cannes or lounging on a yacht in the Mediterranean.

This failure to make contact with the Walenskas bolstered Alice's confidence. She was sure that the Atkinsons, whose name appeared beneath the Walenskas', would not be home; but a woman with a deep smoker's rasp answered after only three rings.

"Is that Mrs Atkinson?" asked Alice, trying to keep her own voice low.

"Yes, it is."

Alice allowed a brief silence: what next? "Um, well, Mrs Atkinson, my name's Alice Armstrong, and I'm sorry to bother you, but I was given your name and number by Mrs Funk, Simone Funk, who said that —"

"Ah, *Simone*!" said Mrs Atkinson, her voice opening in her throat so that Alice could practically see the smile spreading across her face. "How is she, the dear girl?"

"I think very well, Mrs Atkinson. But you see, we're thinking, my husband and I, of employing her, to live in, you see, and to be honest, we're not really accustomed, it's the first time, so I just wanted to ask what your, whether you . . ." Alice trailed off. What did she want to ask?

"Well, you don't need me to tell you what a tremendous gal she is," gushed Mrs Atkinson, who seemed thoroughly to have overcome her initial reserve. "Do you have children?"

"Yes, two."

"And I bet they love her already, don't they, the little darlings?"

"They seem to, yes. But I wondered more about her housekeeping, about that side of things —"

"She's very efficient, Simone. She's a super housekeeper. I really can't say it better than that. She's clever, she's got a very happy disposition, she's kind —"

"She seems quite independent," said Alice.

"Oh yes, that too. Not more than you'd want her to be, no —"

"Of course not," said Alice.

"She's there when you need her. Reliable. Very reliable. But independent, too. Never underfoot."

"No, I sensed that," said Alice. "Did you find it a drawback that she doesn't cook?"

There was a little intake of breath at the other end of the line. "No-o. Not at all," said Mrs Atkinson. "Although, you know, it wasn't ever a question for us, because we *have* a cook, you see. We've always had a cook."

"Right, of course." Alice felt diminished by this news.

"I don't know your circumstances," continued Mrs Atkinson, "but that's really what I'd recommend: a cook and a housekeeper both. Because they're very different positions, aren't they? And they require different temperaments."

"Quite. No, I understand."

"But I'm nattering," said Mrs Atkinson. It was a word that Alice was rather surprised to hear. "Have I answered all your questions about Simone?"

"Well, I suppose, I just — "

"Wonderful, wonderful – lovely chatting with you, dear. Must run. Give her my best. You won't be disappointed." And Mrs Atkinson hung up.

Her last words provoked in Alice a twinge of sorrowful guilt, as she thought of Muriel Leclerc's earnest little chirrup, "You will not be disappoint." She flinched at the prospect of ringing Madame Leclerc to tell her that "the position has been filled". That was the phrase, wasn't it? "I'm afraid the position has been filled." She pictured the woman's crestfallen, anxious face, and dismissed the image at once: there was no time for the mistress of the manor to indulge in sentimentality, she told herself. The Leclercs would find something else, somewhere else. And it was the woman's own fault, wasn't it, for not leaving that dreadful husband? Simone Funk had, after all, had the gumption to get rid of her odious spouse. Yet another point in her favour.

There was no need, Alice decided, in light of Mrs Atkinson's enthusiastic testimonial, to telephone the Beckers in Cologne. Anyway, she didn't have the faintest idea what the time difference might be, and had no desire to rouse the family from their beds for so trifling a matter as a reconfirmation of knowledge she already possessed.

*

Simone Funk moved in among the sunflowers one short week later. In addition to the small suitcase, she brought only one large duffel bag which she hauled from the boot of her Mini. That was all.

"You're welcome to decorate the flat as you like," Alice assured her. "If you have your own pictures, or your own rugs – or even some furniture. We could always store this stuff in the basement if you wanted your own things around you."

"That's all right, dear," said Mrs Funk. "I've always travelled light. I've rented furnished when I haven't lived in, and I don't really have time for *things*, in that way. A rolling stone gathers no moss, I always say."

Alice didn't know whether to be impressed or saddened that a woman in her forties would have accrued no more baggage in life than a couple of cases of clothes.

Mrs Funk seemed to read her mind. "It's exactly how I want it, dear. I've got my Mini, which is my independence, and I like to know I can come and go as I please."

"Quite the opposite of Lady Deeds, then?"

"Yes, indeedy," said Mrs Funk, smiling so very broadly that Alice caught, for the first time, the glimmer of gold in the back of her housekeeper's mouth.

Mrs Funk was to have Wednesdays and Sundays for herself – "Though if you need me, sometimes, on those days," she kindly offered, "I'm flexible, you know." And in principle, except when she was babysitting, her days would end at around six. This arrangement promised to suit both Mrs Funk and the Armstrongs very well.

Alice took her housekeeper out into the garden to meet Davy Jones, who initially raised an eyebrow at his new colleague but then managed to muster a grudging handshake.

"Pleased to meet you, Mr Jones," said Mrs Funk with, Alice thought, impressive sincerity, given Davy's chilly demeanour. "You're responsible for these *mag-ni-fi-cent* flowers, am I right?"

"I do my best," conceded Davy warily.

"It's quite a job for one fellow on his own!" Mrs Funk, to Alice's surprise, reached out and touched Davy's flannel arm in a confidential manner. "But I can see you've got it all under your thumb. Your *green* thumb, I should say."

"Well, thank you," muttered Davy, and again, "I do my best."

"We're very fortunate to have Davy." Alice felt some authoritative encomium was required. "He's built these gardens from the beginning."

"Lady Deeds is very particular about her gardens," said Davy.

"Who wouldn't be?" said Mrs Funk. "And isn't she lucky to have both you and Mrs Armstrong to take care of them in her absence?"

Davy grunted. Alice was grateful enough to flush, prettily, and she turned away to look out at the harbour so as not to let it show.

How had they managed without Simone Funk? In the early months, through the autumn and winter, Alice was to ask this question both silently and aloud, to Teddy, an untold number of times. To Mrs Funk herself Alice put it as a statement, and she tried to refrain from saying it too often, so that Mrs Funk's head would not swell, but sometimes it slipped out of her mouth before she had time to censor herself: "I don't know how we got by without you, Mrs Funk. I just don't know."

She wasn't, it had to be acknowledged, a particularly thorough cleaner – no more thorough than Alice had been on her own – nor was she any good at all in the kitchen (on the few occasions when everyone struggled through leathery steaks and watery cauliflower mush that Mrs Funk had rustled up because Alice had had a late-afternoon appointment, Alice thought guiltily of Mrs Atkinson's reproach – *you need a cook* and *a housekeeper* – and laid the blame not on Mrs Funk, but on the inadequacies of the Armstrong household). But she was an immensely generous and appealing woman, in her earthy sort of way.

Sadie and Martha adored her. Right after she moved in, Mrs Funk had bought each of them, from her own funds, a large soft plastic baby doll with blinking blue eyes and bristly lashes, with moveable limbs, and with a layer of slightly tinted, sculpted plastic hair on its crown. She then proceeded to crochet matching baby's ensembles – blue for Martha's, yellow for Sadie's – lacy petticoats, buttoned dresses, cardigans, sets of booties with little laces, and bonnets that covered the ugly plastic hair and tied in tasselled bows beneath the dolls' chins. It was an immense labour, but she seemed to take pleasure in it, and she crocheted each night in front of the television – in her flat, if Alice and Teddy were home, and in the library with the girls if they were out.

She had a weakness for gossipy picture magazines about film stars and the Royal Family, and she kept Alice abreast of celebrity marriages and salacious scandals while she snapped beans or ironed Teddy's shirts. And she told, both the children and occasionally Alice, extraordinary stories about her life.

Alice couldn't quite piece together the chronology of Simone Funk's autobiography; nor could she gauge, exactly, the age of her housekeeper. For example, it wasn't entirely clear when or for how long she had been married to the villainous Erik Funk, and once there was a veiled reference to an earlier, or later, failed union. She told the girls about her bush childhood in a shack in New South Wales, with no electricity until she was twelve years old, of living with her grandmother and father and four older brothers, who were all bullying and cruel to her, and of how she was saved by her schoolteacher, a single woman "of about the age I am now" who took a proprietorial interest in her. She had left her family at fourteen, she said, to stay in the house of this teacher, and yet she repeatedly insisted that she'd been bad at all academic subjects – "It was all Greek to me!" – and that this was why she had left school at sixteen without her Higher School Certificate (this particular fact was relayed as a cautionary tale, to encourage the girls to do their homework).

She had been a runway model in Melbourne at some point, she claimed, and had been courted by numerous handsome and wealthy bachelors, among them a Greek shipping tycoon with oiled hair and six fingers on each hand, and an Arab sheik who had wanted to meet her father so that he might offer to buy her ("like a pound of liver or a new car") and take her home to join a dozen other wives in his Arabian palace. Martha insisted that Simone Funk *had* taken the sheik back to the Wagga Wagga shack, along the dirt track in his chauffeur-driven Rolls-Royce Silver Shadow, where Simone's father, in his singlet and well into the whisky, had given the millionaire a proper shellacking, pounding the table and saying that no fine Australian sheila was to be bartered away like a sheep, and he had threatened to run Simone's suitor off the property, shotgun in hand.

Alice took these wild tales with a grain of salt – "Try the Pacific Ocean full," said Teddy, when she repeated them to him – but she loved them all the same. There were others, too: Simone Funk had been an air hostess for Qantas for a few years, and while serving coffee to a fat Italian man on a flight from Sydney to Rome had been invited to star in his next film. "Fellini, this was," she said calmly, pausing in her dish-drying long enough to preen her white locks, "and at first I didn't believe him. But he gave me his card. It really was, I swear. When I think of it now . . ."

She'd once been homeless in London, and a sympathetic concierge from the Dorchester (or was it Claridge's?), whom she'd met in a pub, had smuggled her into an empty room in the hotel and allowed her to stay, for free, for a fortnight. She'd lived, at some point, on Heron Island, and had earned a living giving scuba-diving lessons to wealthy tourists – "The gifts they gave me you wouldn't believe," she said, her crinkly eyes wide in their sockets, "pearl necklaces, designer clothes – all kinds of crazy stuff."

And then there were her employers. The Holmeses had bred racehorses, and she'd spent the summers with their five children at the stud farm, riding former Melbourne Cup winners. The Beckers had wanted to take her back to Germany with them, to live in their medieval castle. "But I've had my fill of Europe," she said, "and I know which country's home." The Walenskas were a mixed marriage, he Polish, she Swedish ("An actress, she was. She had a role in an early Bergman film"), and their daughter Elise was "the most beautiful child you ever saw, dressed all the time like a princess, with a tiara in her lovely hair". As for Mrs Atkinson, "She loved talking with you," said Mrs Funk to Alice. "She said you had the kindest voice. It's terribly sad, her husband, only fifty, had a stroke a while back and he's like a vegetable now. Thank goodness they've got a fortune and can afford the proper care. They've built a whole wing onto the house," she added, "a real hospital at home, with nurses round the clock. And their boys are still in school, off boarding, you know, at Winchester, or Rugby . . ."

When she heard *these* stories, about the grandeur of the former Funk households, Alice felt a little nervous. What stories, after all, could be made of the humble Armstrongs, whose impressive surroundings were the bank's indulgence, and whose origins (that little flat in New York City! That grimly ordinary clapboard back in Buffalo!) seemed less noteworthy by far than even Simone Funk's own. Alice wished that she had tales to tell about her life's adventures, if not about a moneyed and titled heritage, but finding nothing suitable, she kept quiet. And sometimes – rarely, but sometimes – she felt a twinge of longing for Africa, who had taken such pleasure in Alice's accounts of Martha and Sadie at the zoo, or of their visit, by ferry, to Luna Park across the harbour. Simone Funk, Alice felt, would not consider such commonplace outings worthy of the telling.

One afternoon in August, Alice answered the telephone to a man with a broad Australian accent, the sort of accent Davy Jones had. The man asked if this was indeed the American Ambassador's residence. Alice assured him that he had quite the wrong number, in spite of her clearly American accent. She was momentarily amused.

For mid-September, Alice planned a surprise party in honour of Teddy's fortieth birthday. She started scheming six weeks ahead of time. It was to be a dinner for fifty guests, with specially set-up round tables in the dining room, the library and the conservatory: two tables to a room, with eight guests at each and ten at the hosts' table. She compiled an invitation list with the help of Ariel Boote-Smith, and tried to include as many of the local luminaries among their acquaintance as possible: three titled couples – two Sirs and a Viscount; a well-known Frenchman who dealt in Far Eastern art; an up-and-coming violinist Alice had met only twice at the Boote-Smiths' (Ariel was quite interested in the arts); and a Cuban woman who claimed to be born of the Spanish nobility, and whose fame derived from the variety and eminence of her lovers. It was said that in her large house in Mosman this woman had a magnificent art collection of her own, each Corot and Matisse and Modigliani a gift from one or other of her men. Teddy and Alice had met her several times on the social circuit and Teddy had said, admiringly, after one encounter, "Isn't she spectacular, for seventy-five? With all that black hair, and her amazing skin! Do you realize, Al, she's one of the great geishas of all time!"

"The hair's out of a bottle and the skin's the work of a clever surgeon," Alice had replied, and then, "I didn't know you were after a geisha, Teddy. You picked the wrong girl." But she still thought he would be pleased and impressed to find Reina Maria Infanta among the crowd feting his fortieth.

The rest of the guest list comprised their regular acquaintances – people from the bank, a few couples they'd met through the girls' school, and a smattering culled from the circuit. Ariel Boote-Smith deemed the final selection "highly appropriate". Mrs Funk, looking it over at the kitchen table, whistled through her teeth. "It's quite the party you're planning, isn't it?"

(Alice had briefly wondered whether it was incumbent upon her to include Simone Funk on this list, but when she mentioned the notion to Ariel, her friend gasped in horrified surprise. "Don't think it for a second, Alice! I thought you'd learned enough, by now, about this type of etiquette." She pronounced "etiquette" very precisely, as though it were still a French word.)

*

Madame Poliakoff glared slightly, in the way she had that made her eyes appear to be too close together. "No, for some years, these are my clients. The best homes in Sydney. Señora Infanta, for example, she is my client six years now. So, we see in my books, make sure we make new menu, yes? Otherwise, your guests cannot tell, are they eating at home, at their party, or at yours, yes?"

"Quite," said Alice. She was proud to think she shared a caterer with her grandest visitors, and was proud, too, to have had the wit to show Madame Poliakoff the list, so as to avoid producing an over-familiar meal. After much debate, it was decided that simplicity was of the essence: they would eat foie gras, "with *sa petite salade*", said Madame Poliakoff, followed by sea bass in a light truffle cream sauce, on a bed of thinly sliced potatoes, surrounded by miniature vegetables: "The tiny courgettes, the tiny beans wrapped like a sheaf, the tiny carrots. And one tiny tomato Provençal. This is very good." For the cake, Madame Poliakoff suggested what she called her cocktail cake, and although Alice shuddered at the name – "No rum," she insisted, "no maraschino cherries!" – her caterer was adamant. "It is very light. Most delicious. Thin layers of sponge, like napoleon cake but sponge, not dry. With cream, and above all with cocktail of fruits, all fresh fruits, with very light glaze."

"What kinds of fruits?" asked Alice.

"All kinds. All fresh. You must trust me for the chef. I know what is most delicious. Do not worry: Mr Armstrong will be amazed. And on cake, for birthday, we put sparklers, yes? More adult —" she pronounced it the French way, *adulte* — "more celebration, than candles. So beautiful, the little sparklers, like a firework in the home."

Alice was more than satisfied by Madame Poliakoff's direction; she was in fact so pleased that she did not notice the expression on Simone Funk's face when the caterer's white van pulled away. It was sour, the corners of her mouth pulled down towards her slightly knobbly chin. It was, on the usually appealing Simone Funk, an unbecoming expression.

"She's a royal nightmare, that one," said Mrs Funk, rising from her chair.

"I beg your pardon?"

"Thinks she's the Queen of Sheba."

"I've always thought of Napoleon, myself," Alice smiled. But Mrs Funk was not amused.

"She comes into your own kitchen and tells you what to eat for your own party, as if it were none of your business? That isn't right, Mrs Armstrong. That isn't right."

"She's the very best caterer in town," Alice said, somewhat defensively. "She's a wonderful cook."

"And thinks herself too good for any of the rest of us, doesn't she?" Mrs Funk snorted. "Pardon my saying so, Mrs Armstrong, but she's looking down her nose at you just as much as at the rest of us. Davy warned me what she was like, so I wasn't surprised, but she didn't even *look* at me to say hello. Maybe that's all right back in Russia where she comes from, but it's not Australian manners, Mrs Armstrong. Everyone's equal in this country, and we're all entitled to respect."

"Absolutely," said Alice. "I don't think she *means* to be difficult – it's just her manner. But you mustn't think . . . I'm sure she had no intention . . ."

"Stuck-up cow. She doesn't know the first thing about me," said Simone Funk with venom.

"No, of course —"

"And I'm worth ten of her. I've been close friends in my life with far more important people than she'll ever even cook for. And I've been friends with tramps, too. I don't hold with snobbery, Mrs Armstrong. It's my upbringing. I just don't hold with it." Mrs Funk put her coffee cup in the sink with a significant clatter and stomped up the back stairs to the privacy of her flat. She was gone for an hour and a half – in the middle of her workday – but when she returned, she made no reference to the scene, nor to her absence. She was again her sunny self, and she even bore discussion of Madame Poliakoff, at later times, with only a slight tightening of her thin lips.

Alice would have liked to discuss Mrs Funk's strange outburst with Teddy – indeed, the impulse was so strong in her that she twice set out to do so – but she had to keep mum about the party. Alice didn't feel she could discuss it with Ariel Boote-Smith, because Ariel had very fixed ideas about the role of servants, and would doubtless think Mrs Funk's outburst a good enough reason to replace her. (Ariel, after all, upon hearing about the trial days of Simone Funk and Muriel Leclerc, had been unable to comprehend why Alice had chosen to employ the former.) By force of Alice's silence and Mrs Funk's seemingly constant goodwill, the latter's fit of pique came swiftly to seem remote and faintly surreal, as if, indeed, Alice had imagined the whole thing.

In those late-August weeks, though, in the run-up to Teddy's birthday, there was also the surprise – not pleasant – of Sadie and the massages. One evening, when Teddy was flopped loose-limbed, jacketless and tie askew in the library, in the black leather club chair that they had come to think of as "Daddy's chair", nursing between his long fingers a tumbler full of gin and tonic with lime and ice (brought to him by Mrs Funk; this was generally her last duty of the day), the girls, as was their wont, came scrambling down the marble steps to leap into his lap and assault him with moist kisses.

"Quietly, quietly, girls," urged Teddy with a sigh. "Daddy's tired tonight. He's had a very long and tiring day."

Sadie sprang from the arm of the chair onto the floor, all pink eagerness, the ends of her brown hair reaching out tentacular from her skull with static electricity. "You want a back massage, Daddy? That'll make you feel better." And without awaiting his reply, she stationed herself behind him and proceeded, with surprising force and agility given the tininess of her hands, to knead the muscles of his shoulders and neck.

"Wow, that's a treat," said Teddy, and then, at once, "where'd you learn to do that?"

"Mrs Funk taught us, ages ago," said Martha, casting envious glances at her younger sister. "We've known for the longest time."

"Sometimes, when she's tired, we take turns for her in front of the telly," Sadie added, still massaging.

Teddy sat up in his chair. As he later told Alice, he didn't have any idea how to respond to this news, but it seemed to him just *wrong*. Sadie, unable to continue her manipulations now that her father had made himself taller, continued, "I'm the best at it. I'm better than Martha. That's what Gary says."

"Gary?" repeated Teddy. "Who's Gary?"

"Gary's the driver who takes us to school," Martha said, in a singsong voice. "You know that, Daddy, really. And he pays Sadie five cents a day to give him a back massage all the way home."

"He *what*?"

"I don't mind, Daddy. It's good because then I never have to sit in the front," Sadie explained. "Which is *horrible*. But Martha sometimes has to. Everybody takes turns but me."

Teddy was on his feet by this time. His shirt was rumpled and half untucked, so that a tail poked out of his waistband like a tongue.

"Now I have to do it more," Martha sighed, "because there aren't so many of us."

"Do what? Do what more?" asked their father, with a squeak in his throat.

"Sit in the front, of course."

"Does your mother know about this?"

The girls looked at each other, and guilt swept across their features like a veil. This was the first intimation that they had done something wrong. First Martha, then Sadie shook her head. Like little nodding flowers.

"Where is your mother? Alice? Alice?" Teddy, usually so placid, yelped like a dog, and Alice came running from the kitchen – wiping flour on her apron, a streak of it across her brow – to hear the story.

*

Arguably, Mrs Funk ought not to have taught the girls this peculiarly adult manoeuvre; and certainly she ought not to have enlisted them to provide massages for her benefit. But Simone Funk's transgression paled and was temporarily forgotten next to the nefarious activities of Gary, the lanky, long-haired ne'er-do-well with his dented blue station wagon. Gary, it transpired, had been paying Sadie five cents a day for weeks – she showed them the jar in which her earnings were hoarded; she was saving up, she said, to buy a ballerina doll like her best friend Michelle's – but even that sordid story was not the end of it. It was, it seemed, a much detested duty for any child to have to sit in Gary's front seat on the way to and from school, because Gary (Alice pictured his sinister chipped tooth) was in the habit of driving with only one hand, while resting the other upon the naked thigh of the little girl whose misfortune it was to be beside him. He didn't, it seemed, venture with his grimy fingers up beneath the girls' skirts, but he did, according to Martha, move his hand back and forth slightly, and he left it there. "It gets so hot, and then your leg's all sweaty," Martha explained calmly. "It's really gross."

Worse still, Teddy and Alice discovered that other little girls had complained to their mothers, and aside from Martha and Sadie, there were now only two other children left in Gary's car pool. But no mother had seen fit to contact Alice; no mother had lodged a formal complaint (doubtless on account of Gary's parentage); and Gary, apparently supremely confident, had not even had the sense to desist from his behaviour as his rounds were depleted. The girls delivered their news with no apparent signs of trauma, but both Teddy and Alice were overwhelmed.

And they argued.

"How could you not have known?" Teddy stormed. "You put them in his car each morning, you're here most days when they get home – Christ, Al, you're their mother. You're supposed to protect them! What have you been doing, what strange la-la land are you living in that you could've just let this happen? It's been going on for months! It's been going on for almost a *year*, for Chrissakes!"

"Why is it all *my* fault?" Alice's face was puffy with tears. "You're their father. I mean, we're *both* responsible. And they never told me; I'm not clairvoyant. Nobody told me anything."

"Did they tell Mrs Funk?"

"How would I know?"

"It matters! If they told her and she didn't let us know, then —"

"Don't be ridiculous. Of course she would have told us. Suddenly you think, because of one bad incident, that everyone is suspect —"

"One 'bad incident'? Is that what you call it? When this pervert has been ferrying our kids around with a hard-on for months —"

"Come on, Teddy. You don't know – they said he never moved his hand beyond their thighs —"

"Are you trying to make excuses for him? I'd wring his neck right now. If he has the gall to show his face tomorrow morning, I'm going to kill him. Literally. I'll kill him."

"I'm not making any excuses. I'm just saying it's not as bad as it could have been, if, I don't know —"

"It's bad enough that all the other mothers knew to pull their kids out of the car pool."

"Not *all* of them. Little Karen and Eliza are still —"

"Right. So what's the time now? Nine forty-five? It's not too late: you call their mothers, you tell them what's going on."

"Why *me*? Why can't *you* do it? How come it's all *my* fault? Besides, no mothers ever called me."

"Is that a reason? Christ, Al, what's wrong with you?"

"I just think you're overreacting."

"Over-reacting? Overreacting?" Teddy had turned an extraordinary shade of red, that obliterated his freckles and clashed with his rusty hair. His nostrils were flared like a horse's, and his brows seemed carried on an electric current. His hands, balled into fists, pulsed with fury. Alice was suddenly afraid, for the first time in all their years together, that he would strike her.

"I'll call. Calm down. I'm going to call right now," she said, as evenly as possible. She didn't want to make any movement that might startle him into action. "I'm going to get the list with their numbers from my desk. And then I'll call. But only if you promise me you'll go put cold water on your face and calm down. You don't want Mrs Funk to hear, do you?"

"I don't give a flying fuck if she does. She's been teaching my daughters how to be sex slaves, for Chrissakes —"

"You really are overreacting now, Teddy. That's enough." Alice was backing to the door.

"Do you actually think she's a fit person to take care of our kids, Al? Do you?"

"I absolutely do," said Alice. "And I don't want to hear another word about it. I'm going to call the other mothers, and from tomorrow I'll take the girls myself. Or Mrs Funk will take them. One way or another, we'll manage. But right now you need to calm down."

Alice called Mrs Newhouse and Mrs Robinson. They were aghast, but remained rational. She also called Gary. Her fingers trembled, but she did it. She knew beforehand, however, that she did not have the courage to confront him. In the event, she landed his mother, Mrs Gordon, the Deputy Principal, who told her that Gary was not at home.

"I see," said Alice, biting her lip so hard she could taste blood. "Perhaps you could tell him, it's Mrs Armstrong here, Martha and Sadie's mother, we've had . . . we've had a change of schedule, and we won't be needing Gary anymore. It works out for me to take the girls myself; it's more practical."

"Perhaps you could discuss it with him tomorrow?" suggested the Deputy Principal.

"Well, no, I don't think so," Alice said. "I realize it's very sudden, but it's from tomorrow. We don't require his services any longer, at all."

"I see." Mrs Gordon's voice was chilly.

"I'll send him a cheque for the rest of the month, but from tomorrow, right away, I'll be taking the girls myself."

There was a brief silence at the other end.

"Thank you, Mrs Gordon. And I'm sorry to have disturbed you so late."

"Yes. I'll pass the message along."

Alice wondered whether, in the silence, Mrs Gordon had contemplated asking what was amiss; she wondered whether Mrs Newhouse had already rung to cancel for Karen, even as Alice was on the phone to Mrs Robinson, or whether the other mother, to Mrs Gordon's inevitable stupefaction, was calling now. It was done, anyway. The girls – she went to check on them – were sound asleep, Sadie hemmed in by half a dozen stuffed animals she couldn't be without, and Martha sprawled on her stomach with one arm dangling, so small and perfect, over the edge of the bed.

*

The incident of the back massages and Gary the paedophile cast a pall over Alice's preparations for the party. Repeatedly, over the next few days, she found herself alone in a room, generally the kitchen, with Simone Funk, wanting to quiz her about the matter of the massages, but not daring. She didn't want to upset the equilibrium of the household, such as it was, and she feared – now that she recalled it – an unaccountable outburst from her employee. The idea that she could not speak or act entirely freely in her own home weighed upon Alice, and she came to dread Mrs Funk's cheery anecdotes and updates on Hollywood starlets.

The guilt she felt about the girls and Gary Gordon was bound, Alice recognized, to disturb her, but she couldn't shake the feeling that Teddy's suspicions of Mrs Funk had somehow, germ-like, contaminated the air. She found herself listening, in the back corridor outside Mrs Funk's flat, when the housekeeper was on the phone. She could sense the strain in her own smile when Mrs Funk told a joke, and could sense, too, the other woman's growing uncertainty in her presence. Alice knew it wasn't fair to give Mrs Funk the cold shoulder; it was childish not to express her grievance openly, confidently, in order that the women might discuss it and move on. But already she had Teddy's unprecedented moodiness to contend with – it wasn't fair, either, that he should continue to hold Alice responsible for the whole mess, but she could tell that he did – and the possibility of overt discord with Mrs Funk was more than she could bear.

In spite of Alice's peculiar behaviour, Mrs Funk remained resolutely cheerful. Perhaps thinking that not all was well between the master and mistress of the manor, she made herself discreet, less present, insofar as she was able. But she harboured, or appeared to harbour, no notion that she might figure in Teddy and Alice's feud: she was just the housekeeper, after all, and was keen to show that in moments of domestic crisis she knew her place. For example, when Alice announced that Gary would not be coming anymore, Mrs Funk merely nodded.

"Got another job, then?" she asked vaguely; and seemed satisfied when Alice said, "Something like that."

So that even as Alice felt a curious unease festering within her in regard to Mrs Funk, she was at the same time grateful. If it had not been for

Mrs Funk's efforts, nothing at Chateau Deeds would have seemed normal at all. If Alice had a luncheon or a meeting, Mrs Funk would pick up the girls from school without complaint. If Alice, after a stony night with Teddy, appeared grumpy in the morning – and in those days, she seemed grumpy every day – Mrs Funk would calmly offer to answer the telephone on her behalf, should it ring, and tell whoever it was that Mrs Armstrong wasn't in. If Alice threw up her hands at the prospect of cooking dinner ("What on earth should we eat? I *hate* having to decide!"), Mrs Funk would propose a simple menu – bangers and mash, say, or roast chicken and salad – and would, if Alice's temper seemed to inspire it, go so far as to offer to cook it herself (an offer which usually returned Alice speedily to her senses).

Alice, who had for months believed that she both liked and needed Mrs Funk, but that she liked her more than she needed her, came to like her less and less, and then to like her not at all; indeed (although she could not rationally have explained why this was so), she reached the conclusion that she now needed her desperately instead. This, then, was the predicament of the mistress of the manor: the discovery, one unlikely morning, that one was in thrall to one's servants, that they had made a servant of oneself.

As the date of Teddy's birthday party approached, Alice proceeded with her plans. The invitations had long been sent, the flowers and wines and tables and chairs ordered. Madame Poliakoff had sent the first bill for a full half – always prepaid – of her services, and the cheque, drawn from Alice's housekeeping money, had been dispatched. Ariel and her husband Jack had made an arrangement with Teddy that would keep him out of the house until the other guests had assembled. The girls, thrilled to be in on the secret of their father's party, had been taken to choose matching dresses and hair ribbons for the evening (they would make an appearance at drinks and then retreat for supper in the nursery with Mrs Funk), and were preoccupied with the matter of their presents. And even Teddy, oblivious to the careful machinations taking place behind his back, was caught up, somehow, in the seeping goodwill that party preparations can engender: he thawed, in his resentment, and began to plant affectionate pecks on Alice's nape, or encircle her waist from behind, as he used to do, quotidian manifestations of love that she had missed not so much in themselves (Alice always found Teddy's lips cold and too wet upon her neck) as for what they meant.

By the weekend before the party – it was to take place on the seventeenth, a Thursday – Alice would have told a confidante, had she only had one (Ariel Boote-Smith, for all her companionship, was Alice's husband's employee's wife, and hence no possible intimate *in that way*), that everything was back to normal. Everything except, of course, her newborn froideur towards Mrs Funk, which, somewhat to Alice's surprise, did not dissipate alongside Teddy's resentment, but rather hardened, into a particular formation: Mrs Funk was now only, to Alice, an employee, justly remunerated for services rendered, but no more to be entrusted with her affections than were Davy, Nigel, or Madame Poliakoff.

It was with disciplined professionalism, then, that on the Saturday night Alice made note of the telephone number where she and Teddy could be reached, at the home of a Japanese couple Teddy had met through business – "We won't have to eat raw fish, will we?" Alice had asked, in the old teasing way they had newly rediscovered – and pressed upon Mrs Funk the importance of the girls' bedtime: "I know they always want to stay up later in front of the TV, and I know sometimes you indulge them, but it disrupts their rhythms, and besides, the programs at night are very unsuitable."

"Right you are, Mrs Armstrong. No worries, no fear —"

"Quite." Alice cut her off. "Have a good night."

The routine of Saturday night was comfortingly familiar, after so many months. Mrs Funk would have retired when Teddy and Alice came home, but she would leave the light under the portico lit, and the light in the front hall on as well. In the beginning, she had turned down their bedspread for them, like in a fancy hotel, but Alice had long ago insisted that this wasn't necessary, with a firmness that indicated it was, moreover, undesired: Alice didn't like to think of Mrs Funk roaming their bedroom in their absence, possibly opening drawers or sampling Alice's perfume. Whether or not Mrs Funk *was* going to snoop, Alice preferred not to be reminded of the possibility.

Sometimes upon returning, when Alice went to check on the girls, she could hear the television in Mrs Funk's flat, halfway down the back stairs; but more often than not the house was quiet, and Alice found the sleeping stillness particularly pleasing. (Teddy, who always went straight to their room, didn't pay attention to such subtleties.) So it was that Saturday night, and Alice, relieved that the motions and currents of Chateau Deeds were at last in order (even if she *had* had to consume raw fish, and felt a little queasy for it), retired contentedly to bed.

Sunday was Mrs Funk's day off, so it was not especially strange for the Armstrongs not to see her. That said, quiet seemed to emanate from her quarters: no radio, no television, no clattering of dishes. Alice stood a while, midmorning, on the back stairs, and cocked an ear.

"She must be sleeping in," she said to Teddy. "I'd tell her we're going out, but it's not worth waking her."

And yet, as the Armstrongs piled into their Ford for the planned drive and picnic in the countryside, Teddy noticed that Mrs Funk's Mini wasn't in its corner by the garage.

"She must have got up with the larks. 'Pipped us to the post,' as Jack Boote-Smith would say. Gone for an outing. Funny duck, isn't she, not even to tell us about it?"

"Don't worry," said Alice. "She'll tell us every last detail tomorrow. How she was waterskiing with the Shah of Iran, or having lunch at the Ritz with Robert Redford . . ."

"Or out shearing sheep in the bush with her bare hands," said Teddy. They laughed, all four of them, and went on their way.

When they returned, however, near dusk, Mrs Funk's Mini was still missing. And she hadn't appeared by the time they went to bed.

"It's very strange," said Alice. "Do you think we should worry?"

"She's a grown woman. Honestly. You'll wake up in the morning and she'll be in the kitchen making coffee."

"It'd be the first time."

"Whatever. You know what I mean. She'll be here."

"Reliable."

"What?"

"That's what Mrs Atkinson said: 'independent, but reliable'."

"Well, there you are."

In the morning, there was still no sign of Mrs Funk, and Chateau Deeds seemed to resonate with her absence. Alice tried to behave as though everything were normal, but she kept picturing Mrs Funk in the tangled wreck of her little red car, or Mrs Funk naked, strangled with a stocking, in a patch of scrubland beyond the city limits. She felt as if any such disaster would be her own – Alice's – fault, for having ceased to care for Simone Funk, for disliking her.

On the way to drop the girls at school, she asked them, eyes carefully trained on the road in front of her, whether Mrs Funk had said anything to them about where she was going.

"I don't know," Martha said, almost whispering.

"What do you mean, sweetheart? Either she said something or she didn't."

"We're not supposed to tell," said Sadie. "We're never supposed to tell."

Alice took a deep breath. "Sadie, love, what did she say? You won't get into trouble for telling Mummy, I promise you."

But Sadie did not answer.

"Come on, girls, I'll have to stop the car otherwise, and you'll both be late for school. Then you really *would* get into trouble, and not with Mummy either, but with your teachers. Don't play games, now. Mummy needs to know."

"She just said she was going out," said Martha. "It wasn't any different from the other times."

"What other times?"

"On Saturdays, when you and Daddy are out, Mrs Funk needs to go out, too. 'A lady needs a little fun,' she says. 'You'll understand when you get older.'" Martha imitated Mrs Funk's inflections perfectly.

"I see." Alice had to concentrate very hard on the road. She drove slowly. "When she needs to go out, where does she go?"

"I don't know, Mummy." Martha sounded annoyed. "She reads to us and tucks us in and tells us where your phone number is, and then she tells us to go to sleep. So we do."

"Of course you do, dear. It was just the right thing. But if that ever happens to you again, with anyone, you go right to the phone, sweetie, and you call me straight away, and Mummy and Daddy will come home at once."

"You wouldn't need to. I'm a big girl now. Mrs Funk says so. I'm old enough to take care of us perfectly well."

"Almost eight isn't that big, sweetheart. You'll have plenty of time to take care of yourself in life, but just now, Mrs Funk was supposed to take care of you. Mummy and Daddy wouldn't have left you otherwise. Did she say anything about where she was going? Think hard, girls – anything?"

"She has a boyfriend," Sadie said.

"She has lots of boyfriends, dummy," said her sister. "She says, 'A lady needs a bloke like a fish needs a bicycle. But sometimes a fish needs a bicycle.' And then she laughs."

"Was she going out with her boyfriend, then?"

"I don't know, Mummy, I told you. She just said she was going out."

When Alice arrived back at Chateau Deeds, she went straight to Mrs Funk's flat and tried the door. It was not locked. Inside, everything was as

Alice had arranged it, months before, before she had even met Mrs Funk: the sunflower curtains were half open, the window cracked. Dust motes danced in the morning sun. The bed was neatly made; the surfaces were bare. The fridge was empty except for half a shrivelled lime, some flat tonic water, and a small bottle of milk, half drunk, with the foil cap stuck on haphazardly. The drawers rolled lightly out of the dresser, weighted only by their shelf paper. The towels in the bathroom – Lady Deeds' towels, the yellow set – were missing. Even the wastepaper baskets were empty. Alice saw again Mrs Funk's suitcase and her duffel bag, heard again her insistence that a rolling stone gathers no moss. But why? Why now?

Alice, in a panic, ran to the dining-room sideboard and counted the Deeds' silver plate, but none, as far as she could see, was missing. She ran up to her own room and rifled through her underwear drawer, examining the jewellery, but it all seemed to be there, with the exception of a little pearl ring she couldn't recall seeing recently: it might simply have been mislaid. She stood in the doorway of the drawing room and tried to determine whether all the china shepherdesses were smiling back at her, and while she couldn't be absolutely certain without the help of the inventory list, it did appear that they were present in their usual superabundance.

She called Teddy at work. "She's done a runner," she said. "That's what it looks like."

"Mrs Funk has done a bunk?" said Teddy. "Now *that's* news." He whistled through his teeth. "What's the damage? What did she steal, the canny old trout?"

"I'm not sure she took anything. A set of towels, I think. And maybe my pearl ring from Aunt Vera, but I can't be sure. I haven't checked everything, but it all looks okay."

"When did she sneak out? Sunday morning early, I guess."

Alice did not have the heart to tell him, in light of the Gary Gordon incident, about Mrs Funk's Saturday-night forays. She would tell the girls not to mention it either. "Something like that. Must have been."

Teddy paused. "Are you upset?"

"It's very inconvenient." Alice thought for a moment. "But I don't know if I'm upset. We owed her two weeks' pay."

"She doesn't seem to care."

"No, I guess not."

"Call that lady, Al. Why don't you call that lady she worked for before?"

"The high and mighty Mrs Atkinson, who has a whole hospital in her house? I suppose."

"It's worth finding out, you know, if, I don't know . . ."

"Maybe she left because we weren't posh enough? Maybe we didn't provide enough fodder for her stories – no horses, no fortune, no medieval castles; and Chateau Deeds doesn't even belong to us."

"Al, why don't you call the lady?"

When Alice called Mrs Atkinson, however, she found, at the far end of the line, a Philippine gentleman whom she initially took for the Atkinsons' butler, but who seemed to be trying to tell her that he knew nobody named Atkinson, that he rented his apartment furnished by the week, and had only been in Sydney for a month and a half.

"Thank you for your help, sir," Alice said at last, "and goodbye."

The girls seemed to swallow Mrs Funk's disappearance with the equanimity they reserved for all adult absurdities. Alice told them that Miss Dewar would come to sit for them on the night of the surprise party, and they were delighted, in much the same way they were delighted, sometimes, to recover a forgotten but beloved toy from under the bed or from the bottom of their toy box.

Alice went ahead with the party with a light heart, although on the night before, she dreamed that Mrs Funk turned up among the guests, in a black silk cocktail dress of Alice's, with her white hair shining like a halo.

When Madame Poliakoff, upon arriving at Chateau Deeds on Thursday afternoon, inquired about the housekeeper, Alice replied, as imperiously as possible, that Mrs Funk had proven unsatisfactory and was no longer employed in the Armstrong household. She hoped that she said this with sufficient sting to imply that Madame Poliakoff, too, might be dispensable, were her services not up to snuff; but the Russian remained uncowed.

"Is very difficult," she said, shaking her coppery head. "Many of the finest houses have these problems with the staff. I think is because there is no training, not as in Europe, where training is very good."

"You may be right," Alice agreed.

"I could see, looking at this woman, how she is acting." Madame Poliakoff clicked her tongue. "I am not surprised. But we make marvellous party, yes? So let me explain . . ." And she was off.

A fortnight after Teddy's birthday party – at which, to his supreme pleasure, Señora Infanta kissed him roundly on the lips and pressed her ample, if aged, décolletage against his bony chest – two plainclothes policemen appeared at the front door of Chateau Deeds. The first, a burly man wearing an ugly patterned sweater in spite of the spring warmth, asked if this was indeed the American Ambassador's residence.

"I'm afraid not, gentlemen. How silly – surely you can check that address in your files?"

"But you are an American, madam?"

"Yes, obviously. But Teddy, my husband, is a banker. I can tell you, I've *met* the American Ambassador, and I've met his wife, too, and if you want to find them —"

"Very good, madam," the other, balder man cut in, with a nervous lick of his lips. "But does a Simone Streatham live here?"

"Who?"

"Do you employ a housekeeper by the name of Simone Streatham?"

"Simone Funk, you mean?"

"I don't know about that, madam. We're looking for a Simone Streatham."

"What has she done?"

"Bad cheques, madam. And credit-card fraud. A nasty character. You'll be wanting to tell us where she is. Can we come through, madam?"

"But Mrs Funk is gone," Alice said, feeling her first, belated pang of fondness for the woman. "She disappeared – *poof* – like that. About two weeks ago. It was quite a shock. We just woke up one Sunday morning and she was gone."

"No forwarding address, madam?" asked the burly man, whose belly pressed firmly against his ugly sweater.

"You don't usually leave an address when you intend to disappear, do you?" Alice answered rather crossly. It occurred to her that she was not even certain these men were policemen. She felt almost glad that Mrs Funk had escaped them. She felt almost envious. Simone Funk was reinventing herself, inventing her life as she wanted it to be. "It's a shame," she continued. "And I'm sorry I can't help you further. I have no idea, not the foggiest, where she is."

As the two men turned, reluctantly, and sloped back around the gravel drive towards their car, pausing to ogle the statue of Pan on his fountain, Alice called out to them, half from perversity and half in genuine sorrow, "It's a real shame. She was a very good housekeeper."

Alice Armstrong did not seek to replace Mrs Funk. She and Teddy both agreed that it was not ideal to have an employee living in one's house. They knew, now, what it meant to live in Chateau Deeds, to live in it properly, as Lady Deeds would have had them do it, and in spite of the grandeur of the unfolding rooms, in spite of the elegant portico and trickling fountain, in spite of the rose garden and the side lawn and the miniature orchard, the walled garden and the aviary and the garage that resembled stables, with its carefully covered Bentley inside, in spite of these manifold advantages, they decided they did not want to live any longer in Chateau Deeds.

"It makes us into people we aren't," observed Alice. "Into people I don't want to be."

When, a couple of months into the new year, the lease came up, the Armstrong family did not renew. They moved to a charming but unspectacular modern house in Woollahra, with no view and only a single rose bush, without retainers or furniture, without even a service flat, but with, instead, a stand of bamboo, a banana tree, and a turquoise, kidney-shaped swimming pool. Martha and Sadie were, as ever, quite calm about the transfer, and did not even appear to miss their splendid playroom. "A swimming pool is loads better," observed Martha sagely, "all the girls at school have them. Now we can be proper Australians, and swim like fish."

Acknowledgements

With many thanks to the American Library in Paris, where this was written, now some years ago; and to my wonderful publisher Jemma Birrell, and my amazing agent, Sarah Chalfant. Grateful always to my family – James, Livia and Lucian – and to my sister Elizabeth.